Claude's Confession

Claude's Confession

Émile Zola

MINT EDITIONS

Claude's Confession was first published in 1865.

This edition published by Mint Editions 2021.

ISBN 9781513282145 | E-ISBN 9781513287164

Published by Mint Editions®

MINT
EDITIONS

minteditionbooks.com

Publishing Director: Jennifer Newens
Design & Production: Rachel Lopez Metzger
Project Manager: Micaela Clark
Translation By: George D. Cox
Typesetting: Westchester Publishing Services

Contents

I. A Mansarde in the Latin Quarter   7

II. A Poet's Longings   10

III. The Young Harvest-Girl   12

IV. Temptation   13

V. Paquerette   17

VI. Despair   20

VII. Laurence   21

VIII. A Mission from on High   25

IX. The Course of Reformation   26

X. The Embroidery Strip   29

XI. On the Way to the Ball   32

XII. The Public Ball   40

XIII. An Acceptance of Reality   45

XIV. Jacques and Marie   48

XV. Biting Poverty   55

XVI. Reminiscences   59

XVII. Claude's Love   64

XVIII. Jacques' Supper   69

XIX. A Trip to the Country 75

XX. A Bitter Avowal 85

XXI. A Horrible Proposition 89

XXII. The Shadows on the Wall 93

XXIII. Practical Advice 104

XXIV. Sad Reflections 114

XXV. The Fair 116

XXVI. At Marie's Bedside 127

XXVII. Marie's Death 130

XXVIII. Laurence's Departure 138

XXIX. Conclusion 145

I

A Mansarde in the Latin Quarter

Winter is here: the air in the morning becomes fresher, and Paris puts on her mantle of fog. This is the season of social soirées. Chilly lips search for kisses; lovers, driven from the country, take refuge beneath the mansardes, and, huddling together before the hearth, enjoy, amid the noise of the rain, their eternal spring.

As for me, I live in sadness: I have the winter without the spring, without a sweetheart. My garret, away up a damp staircase, is large and irregular; the corners lose themselves in the gloom, the bare and slanting walls make of the chamber a sort of corridor which stretches out in the form of a bier. The wretched furniture, the narrow planks, ill fitted and painted a horrible red color, crack funereally when they are touched. Shreds of faded damask hang from the canopy of the bed, and the curtainless window opens upon a huge black wall, never changing and always repulsive.

In the evening, when the wind shakes the door and the walls are dimly outlined by the flame of my lamp, I feel a sad and icy weariness press upon me. I pause before the expiring fire on the hearth, before the ugly brown roses on the wall paper, before the faïence vases in which the last flowers have faded, and I imagine I hear everything complain of solitude and poverty. This complaint is heart-rending. The entire mansarde demands of me laughter, the riches of its sisters. The hearth exacts a huge, joyous blaze; the vases, forgetting the snow, sigh for fresh roses; the very air speaks to me of flaxen hair and white shoulders.

I listen and cannot help feeling sorrowful. I have no chandelier to suspend from the ceiling, no carpet to hide the irregular and broken planks. And, when my chamber refuses to smile save upon a beautiful white curtain, upon plain but shining furniture, I grow more sorrowful still because I cannot satisfy it. Then it seems to me more deserted and miserable than ever: the wind comes in colder gusts, the gloom grows denser; the dust gathers in heaps on the floor, the wall paper tears showing the plaster. There is a general pause, and, in the silence, I hear the sobs of my heart.

Brothers, do you remember the days when life for us was a dream? We had friendship, we had visions of love and glory. Do you recall those cool evenings in Provence, when, as the stars came out, we sat down in the furrows still glowing with the heat of the sun? The crickets chirped; the harmonious breath of summer nights enveloped our chat. All three of us let our lips say what our hearts thought, and, in our simplicity, we adored queens, we crowned ourselves with laurels. You told me your dreams, I told you mine. Then, we deigned to come back to earth. I confided to you my plan of life, consecrated to toil and struggles. Feeling the wealth of my mind, I was pleased at the idea of poverty. You were ascending, like me, the stairway of the mansardes, you hoped to nourish yourselves on high thoughts; in your ignorance of the reality, you seemed to believe that the artist in his sleepless night gains the bread of the morrow.

At other times, when the flowers were sweeter, the stars more radiant, we caressed visions of loveliness. Each of us had his sweetheart. Yours—do you recollect?—brown and laughing girls, were queens of the harvest and vintage; they played about, decked with ears of grain and bunches of grapes, and ran along the paths, carried away in the whirl of their turbulent youth. Mine, pale and blonde, had the royalty of the lakes and clouds; she walked languidly, crowned with verbenas, seeming at each step about to quit the earth.

Do you remember, brothers, that last month we went thus to dream amid the fields and draw the courage of man from the holy faith of the child? I was weary of dreaming, I thought myself strong enough for reality. Five weeks have passed since I left our broad district, fertilized by the hot breath of the south. I grasped your hands, said adieu to our favorite field, and was the first to go in search of the crown and the sweetheart reserved by God for our twentieth year.

"Claude," you said to me at the moment of departure, "you are about to begin the struggle. To-morrow, we shall not be beside you as formerly, imparting to you hope and courage. You will find yourself alone and poor, having only recollections to people and gild your solitude. The way is rough, people tell us. Go, however, since you thirst for life. Remember your plans: be firm and loyal in action, as you were in your dreams; live in the garrets, eat your dry bread, smile at want. As a man, do not jeer at the ignorance of the child, but accept the hard labor of the grand and the beautiful. Suffering elevates a man, and tears are dried one day when one has greatly loved. Have courage and wait for us. We will console you and scold you from here. We cannot follow you now, for we do not possess your strength; our dream is yet too seductive for us to change it for reality."

Scold me, brothers, and console me. I am only commencing to live, and I am already very sad. Ah! how joyous was the mansarde of our dreams! How the window sparkled in the sunshine, and how poverty and solitude rendered life there studious and peaceful! Want had for us the luxury of light and smiles. But do you know how ugly a real mansarde is? Do you know how cold one is when one is alone, without flowers, without white curtains upon which to rest the eyes? Light and gayety pass by without entering, fearing to venture amid the gloom and silence.

Where are my fields and my brooks? Where are my setting suns, which gilded the tops of the poplars and changed the rocks into sparkling palaces? Have I deceived myself, brothers? Am I only a lad who would be a man before his time? Have I had too great confidence in my strength, and should I still be dreaming beside you?

The day is breaking. I have passed the night before my extinguished fire, looking at my poor walls and relating to you my first sufferings. A wan light illuminates the roofs, a few flakes of snow fall slowly from the pale, sad sky. The awakening of great cities is tumultuous. I hear, coming up to me, those street murmurs which resemble sobs.

No; this window refuses me the sunlight, this floor is damp, this mansarde is deserted. I cannot love, I cannot work here.

II

A Poet's Longings

You are irritated by my lack of courage, you accuse me of coveting velvet and bronze, of not accepting the holy poverty of the poet. Alas! I love broad curtains, candelabra, marble upon which the chisel has left the impress of its powerful caresses. I love everything that shines, everything that has beauty, grace and richness. I need princely dwellings, or, rather, the fields with their carpets of fresh and perfumed moss, their draperies of leaves, their wide horizons of light. I prefer the luxury of God to the luxury of men.

Pardon, brothers, for silk is so soft, lace so light; the sun laughs so gayly in gold and crystal!

Let me dream; have no fear for my pride. I wish to hear your strong and cheering words, to embellish my mansarde with gayety, to illuminate it with noble thoughts. If I feel too lonely, I will create for myself an ideal sweetheart who, responsive to my call, will run to kiss me on the forehead after the accomplishment of my task. If the floor be cold, if I have no bread, I will forget winter and hunger in feeling my heart warm. In one's twentieth year it is easy to be the artisan of one's joy.

The other night, the voice of the winds was melancholy, my lamp was dying, my fire was extinguished; sleeplessness had troubled my mind, pale phantoms were wandering about me in the gloom. I was afraid, brothers, I felt myself weak, I shed tears. The first ray of dawn drove off the nightmare. Now, the obstacle is no longer in me. I accept the struggle.

I wish to live in a desert, hearing only my heart, seeing only my dream. I desire to forget men, to question myself and reply. Like a young wife whose bosom quivers with a mother's anxiety, the poet, when he thinks an idea awakening in him, should have an hour of ecstasy and reflection. He runs to shut himself up with his dear burden, fears to believe in his good fortune, interrogates his soul, hopes and doubts in turn. Then, when a sharper pain tells him that God has made his mind fruitful, for long months he shuns the crowd, giving himself entirely to the love of the masterpiece which Heaven has confided to him.

Let him hide himself, and enjoy like a miser the anguish of production; to-morrow, in his pride, he will come forth to demand caresses for the fruit of his mind.

I am poor; I should live alone. My pride would suffer from commonplace consolations, my hand wishes to press only those of my equals. I am ignorant of the world, but I feel that Want is so cold she must freeze the hearts around her, and that, being the sister of Vice, she is timid and ashamed when she is noble. I carry my head aloft and do not mean to lower it.

Poverty and Solitude, be you then my guests. Be my guardian angels, my muses, my companions with harsh but encouraging voices. Make me strong, give me the science of living, tell me the cost of my daily bread. May your vigorous caresses, so sharp that they seem like wounds, force me towards the good and the just. I will relight my lamp during these winter nights, and I will feel you both beside me, icy and silent, bending over my table, dictating to me the hard truth. When, weary of gloom and silence, I put by my pen and curse you, your melancholy smiles will, perhaps, make me doubt my dreams. Then your serene and sad peace will render you so beautiful that I will take you for my sweethearts. Our loves shall be as serene and deep as you; the lovers of sixteen will envy the bitter pleasure of our fruitful kisses.

But, nevertheless, brothers, it would be delightful to me to feel the purple upon my shoulders, not to drape myself with it before the crowd, but to live more generously beneath the rich and superb tissue. It would be delightful to me to be king of Asia, to dream night and day upon a bed of roses in one of those fairy-like dwelling-places, harems of flowers and sultanas. The marble baths with perfumed fountains, the galleries of honeysuckles supported by silver trellises, the immense halls with ceilings sown with stars, do not these constitute the palace which the angels should build for each young man of twenty? Youth wishes at its festival all that sings, all that shines. When the first kiss is given, the fiancée should be covered with lace and jewels, and the nuptial couch, borne by four golden and marble fairies, should have a canopy of precious stones and sheets of satin.

Brothers, brothers, do not scold me, for I wish to be wise. I shall love my garret and think no more of my palaces. Oh! how fresh and passionate life would be in them!

III

The Young Harvest-Girl

I toil and hope. I pass the days seated at my little table, putting aside my pen for long hours to caress some ideal blonde whom the ink would soil. Then, I resume my work, decking my heroines with the rays of my dreams. I forget the snow and the empty closet. I live I know not where, perhaps in a cloud, perhaps amid the down of an abandoned nest. When I write a phrase sprucely and coquettishly draped, I imagine I see angels and hawthorns in bloom.

I have the holy gayety of toil. Ah! how foolish I was to be sad, and how deceived I was in thinking myself poor and alone! Yesterday my chamber was hideous; now it smiles upon me. I feel around me friends whom I cannot see, but who are legion and who all put out their hands to me. So great is their number that they hide from me the walls of my den.

Poor little table, when Despair shall touch me with her wing, I will always seat myself before you and bend over the white paper on which my dream fixes itself only after having given me a smile.

Alas! I must have, nevertheless, a shade of reality. I surprise myself sometimes uneasy, wishing for a joy that I cannot shape. Then, I hear something like a complaint from my heart: it tells me that it is always cold, always famished, and that a mad dream can neither warm nor satisfy it. I wish to content it. I will go out to-morrow, no longer isolating myself in myself, but gazing at the windows, telling it to make its choice from among the beautiful ladies. Then, from time to time, I will take it back beneath the chosen balcony. It will carry away from it a glance to feed on, and, for a week, will no longer feel the winter. When again it shall cry famine, a new smile shall appease it.

Brothers, have you never imagined that, on a certain autumn evening, you met amid the grain fields a brunette of sixteen? She smiled upon you as she flitted by, then was lost among the wheat heads. That night you dreamed of her, and, on the morrow, at the same hour, took the path from the town. The dear vision passed, smiled again, leaving you a new dream for your next sleep. Months, years elapsed. Every day your famished heart was satisfied with a smile and never desired more. An entire lifetime would not be long enough for you to exhaust the glance of the young harvest-girl.

ÉMILE ZOLA

IV

Temptation

Last evening, I had a bright fire on the hearth. I was rich enough to have two candles, and had lighted them both, regardless of the morrow.

I surprised myself singing, as I prepared for a night of toil. The mansarde laughed to find itself warm and luminous.

As I sat down, I heard on the stairway the sound of voices and hurried steps. Doors opened and shut. Then, amid the silence that ensued, stifled cries came up to me. I sprang to my feet, vaguely disturbed, and listened. The noise ceased. I was about to resume my chair, when some one ran up-stairs and called out to me that a woman, my neighbor, had a nervous attack. My help was asked. I held the door open, but saw only the dark and gloomy stairway.

I put on a warmer coat and went down, forgetting even to take one of my candles. On the floor below I stopped, not knowing what room to enter. I did not hear a sound; I was surrounded by thick darkness. At last I saw a thin thread of light through a half open door. I gave the door a push.

The chamber was the sister of mine: large, irregular and out of repair. But, as I had left my mansarde in a flood of flame and brightness, the gloom and cold of this place filled my heart with pity and sadness. Damp air struck against my face; a miserable candle, burning on one corner of the mantelpiece, flickered in the blast from the stairway, without permitting me at first to see the objects before me.

I had paused upon the threshold. Finally I distinguished the bed: the sheets, thrown off and twisted, had slipped to the floor; scattered garments lay about on the coverlet.

In the midst of these rags was stretched out a vague, white form. I should have thought I saw a corpse, if the candle had not given me occasional glimpses of a hand hanging out of the bed and agitated by rapid convulsions.

By the pillow was an old woman. Her unfastened gray hair fell in stiff locks over her forehead, her hastily put on dress showed her yellow and wasted arms. She had her back towards me, was holding the head and hid from me the face of the woman on the bed.

The quivering body, watched over by this horrible old woman, gave me a sudden feeling of disgust and fright. The motionlessness of their countenances gave them fantastic dimensions, their silence made one almost doubt that they were alive. I thought for an instant that I was witnessing one of those terrible scenes of the witches' Sabbath, when the sorceresses suck the blood of young girls, and, throwing them ghastly and wrinkled into the arms of Death, rob them of their youth and freshness.

The noise I made at the door caused the old woman to turn her head. She let the body she was supporting fall heavily; then, she advanced towards me.

"Ah! Monsieur," she said, "I thank you for having come. Old people fear the winter nights, and this room is so cold that, perhaps, I would not have been able to leave it in the morning. I have been watching a long while, and when one eats but little, one needs more sleep. Besides, the crisis is over. You will have to wait only until this girl awakens. Good night, Monsieur."

The old woman went away, and I was alone. I shut the door, and, taking up the candle, approached the bed. The girl extended upon it seemed about twenty-four. She was plunged in that deep stupor which follows nervous convulsions. Her feet were drawn up beneath her; her arms, still stiff and wide open, were thrown over the edges of the bed. I could not at first judge of her beauty: her head, thrown backward, was concealed by her flood of hair.

I took her in my arms, straightened out her limbs and placed her upon her back. Then I drew away the hair from her face. She was ugly: her closed eyes had no lashes, her temples were low and retiring, her mouth large and sunken. Premature old age had effaced the outlines of her features and left upon her whole countenance an imprint of lassitude and avidity.

She was sleeping. I heaped over her feet all the rags within my reach; then I raised her head by putting under it more old clothes which I had found and rolled into a bundle. My science being limited to these cares, I decided to wait until she awoke. I feared lest she might have another attack, fall and wound herself.

I examined the garret. On entering I had noticed a strong perfume of musk, which, mingling with the sharp odor of the dampness, struck strangely upon the sense of smell. Upon the mantelpiece was a row of vials and little pots, still greasy with aromatic oils. Above hung a cracked

ÉMILE ZOLA

looking-glass, with the amalgam at the back gone in broad patches. In addition, the walls were bare. Many things lay about on the floor: satin shoes down at the heel, dirty linen, faded ribbons, rags of lace. As I went along, scattering the tatters with my foot to make a passage for myself, I came across a handsome dress of blue silk, ornamented with bows of velvet. It had been thrown into a corner among the other gewgaws, rolled up, rumpled, stained yet with the mud of the town. I raised it and hung it on a nail.

Weary and finding no chair, I sat down on the foot of the bed. I began to understand where I was. The girl still slept; she was now plainly visible. I thought I had made a mistake in declaring her ugly, and looked at her with greater attention. An easier sleep had brought to her lips a vague smile; her features were relaxed; her past suffering had given a sort of gentle and sad beauty to her ugliness. She reposed, sorrowful and resigned. Her soul seemed to have taken advantage of her rest to mount to her face.

I was amid unclean want, a strange assemblage of blue silk and filth. This garret was the infamous den of famished luxury selling its satiety; this girl was one of those old wretches of twenty, no longer having anything of the woman about them but the fatal stamp of their sex, vending that mortality which Heaven has left them in withdrawing their souls. How could so much slime be in a single being, so many stains on a single heart! God roughly smites His creature when He allows her to tear her robe of innocence and assume the wretched garments of vice! In our visions of love, we never dreamed that some night we should find a miserable bed in a garret full of gloom, and, upon that bed, a girl of the gutter, asleep and half-clad!

The unfortunate creature was evidently under the caressing wing of a dream; gentle and regular breath escaped from her lips; over her languidly closed eyelids at times ran a faint quiver. I leaned upon the bed; my glance could not loosen itself from that pale face, beautiful with a strange beauty. I know not what fascination was exerted upon me by this peaceful sleep of vice, these faded features, stamped in their repose with an angelic mildness. I said to myself that this slumbering girl was receiving a visit from her sixteenth year, and that thus purity itself was before me. This thought filled my mind; if any other mingled with it I did not know it. I no longer felt the cold, but I trembled. My veins throbbed with an unknown fever. My reverie rambled on, more uneasy and more sorrowful.

The girl uttered a sigh, and turned over. She threw back the coverlet, exposing her bust.

My dreams had shown me only chaste statues, always veiled by dazzling brightness. I had seen but the arms of washerwomen, gayly beating their linen. Sometimes, perhaps, my glance had strayed over the white and delicate neck of a danseuse, when, getting the better of my heart, I had felt my thoughts troubled by the sweep of her flaxen tresses.

This roughly uncovered bust made me blush, and filled me with such anguish that I was on the point of weeping. I was ashamed for the young woman's sake; I felt my purity departing as I gazed at her. Nevertheless, I could not turn away my eyes; I followed the gentle undulations of her breast, and was dazzled by its whiteness. My senses were still silent; my mind alone was intoxicated. My impressions had a charm so strange that I can now compare them only to the holy horror that shook me the day I beheld a corpse for the first time. My imagination had represented death to me. But when I saw that bluish face, that black and open mouth, when destruction showed itself in its energetic grandeur, I could not withdraw my glances from the dead, for I was quivering with a sorrowful delight, I was attracted by I know not what glimmer of reality.

Thus, the first bare throat held me palpitating with an emotion I am unable to define.

And it was a bust bruised by harsh caresses upon which my eyes rested! Ah! when I now think of it, of that frightened ecstasy which restrained my breath, when I again see myself bent over that infamous couch, uneasy and blushing, I ask myself with anguish who will restore to me that first glance that I may bend and blush over the couch of purity! I ask myself who will restore to me the instant when the veil falls from the shoulders of the bride, when the bridegroom comprehends that the choicest gift of Heaven is his and bows his head, dazzled by the knowledge! I have drunk to intoxication from a perilous cup; I shall never realize what splendor a bride has in the eyes of a young and innocent husband.

The girl awoke and smiled, without seeming astonished to find me near her. Her smile was vague, as if addressed to a crowd, as if weary of being upon her lips. She did not speak, but put out her arms towards me.

In the morning, when I returned to my garret, I found my candles entirely burned away and the fire on my hearth long dead. The chamber was cold and sombre: I no longer had either flame or brightness.

V

PAQUERETTE

B rothers, where is the sweetheart, queen of the lakes and clouds, or the harvest brunette whose glance is so deep as to suffice for a life of love?

Well, all is over: I have belied my youth; I am the fiancé of vice. The remembrance of my first hour of love is closely bound to that of an infamous den, of a couch over which strange kisses float. When, during the May nights, I shall evoke my fiancée, I shall see arise a half-clad, cynical girl, awaking and putting out her arms towards me. This pale and stained spectre will be a participant in all my love affairs. It will stand between my mouth and that of my bride, claiming the kisses of my soiled lips. When I am asleep, it will visit me in a horrible dream. When my sweetheart shall whisper in my ear some delicious word, it will be there to tell me that it was the first to talk thus to me. When I shall lean my head upon the shoulder of my bride, it will present to me its shoulder on which I once reposed. Thus it will ever freeze my heart with the accursed remembrance of our betrothal.

Yes, that night has sufficed to deprive me of supreme peace. My first kiss has not awakened a soul. I have not felt the holy ignorance of pure caresses, my timid lips have not found lips as timid as themselves. I shall never experience that simple playfulness, that innocence of a couple who know not the ways of the world. They tremble, embrace, and weep for joy. But, as they kiss each other, hesitatingly, they realize that they are one, that their hearts beat in unison, and that God has joined them for the voyage of life.

Then, when this knowledge has come, when they have in a kiss divined the law of the Omnipotent, what must be their delight to owe to each other this revelation, this infinitude of joy! They have participated in a common blessing: they have put on their white robes and now are clad like the cherubim. Mingling their very breath, smiling with the same smile, they repose in their union. Holy hour, in which hearts beat more freely, finding a heaven to which they can ascend. Sainted hour, in which ignorant love suddenly learns the full measure of its strength, believes itself the master of the universe and is intoxicated with its first flight. Brothers, may God keep for you that hour, the remembrance of which perfumes one's entire life. It will never be mine.

Such is fate. It is rare that two pure hearts meet; nearly always one heart of any twain can no longer give its ecstasy in its flower. To-day, most young men of twenty like ourselves, who are eager to love, lacking the power to force the bars and bolts of honest houses, hasten to the wide open doors of boudoirs easier of access. When we ask upon what shoulders we shall lean our heads, fathers hide their daughters and push us into the gloom of the lanes. They cry out to us to respect their children, who will some day be our wives; they prefer for them, instead of our first caresses, those learned elsewhere.

Hence how few keep their early love for their brides, how few, in the desert of their youth, refuse the companions into whose society they are driven by the singular behavior of parents! Some, foolish and wicked lads, glory in their shame; they drag their ignoble flirtations before the public eye. Others, when the soul awakes at the first summons of the sweetheart, are filled with overwhelming sorrow on vainly interrogating the horizon and at not knowing where to find the rightful claimant of the heart. They go straight ahead, staring at the balconies, leaning towards each youthful visage: the balconies are deserted, the youthful visages remain veiled. Some night an arm is slipped within their own, a voice makes them start. Already weary and despairing, unable to discover the angel of love, they follow the spectre.

Brothers, I do not wish to make an excuse for my fault, but let me say that it is strange to cloister purity and permit dissipation to walk in the glare of the sun with uplifted head. Let me deplore this distrust of love, which creates a solitude around the lover, and this guarding of virtue by vice, which causes a young man to encounter shame before reaching the door of innocence. He who yields to temptation may well say to his bride: "I am unworthy of you, but why did you not come to my rescue? Why did you not meet me in the flowery fields, before all those by-ways, each nook of which has its priestess? Why were you not the first to greet my eyes, thus sparing yourself in sparing me?"

On returning home this evening, I found upon the stairway the old woman of the other night. She was toilsomely ascending in front of me, aiding herself with the cord and placing both feet on each step. She turned around.

"Well, Monsieur, is your patient better?" she asked. "She no longer shivers, I imagine, and you yourself do not seem to have suffered from the cold. Ah! I well knew that a young man could take better care of a handsome girl than an old woman."

She laughed, showing her empty mouth. The politeness of this aged wretch who had led a gay life made me blush.

"You need not color so!" she added. "I have seen others as proud as yourself enter without shame and depart singing. Youth loves to laugh, and girls who play the wise one are fools. Ah! if I were only fifteen again!"

I had reached my door. She caught me by the arm as I was about to go in, and continued:

"I had flaxen hair then, and my cheeks were so fresh that my admirers nicknamed me Pâquerette. If you had seen me, you would have been astonished. I lived on the ground floor, in a nest of silk and gold. Now, I lodge under the eaves. I have only to descend to go to the cemetery. Ah! your friend Laurence is happy: she is as yet but in the fourth story."

So the girl was called Laurence. I had been ignorant even of her name.

VI

DESPAIR

I resumed my work, but with repugnance, and was weary from the commencement. Now that I had lifted a corner of the veil, I had neither the courage to let it fall again nor the boldness to draw it away altogether. When I seated myself at my table, I leaned sadly on my elbows, letting the pen slip from my fingers and muttering: "What is the good!" My intelligence seemed worn out; I dare not re-read the few phrases I had written; I no longer felt that joy of the poet, whom a happy rhyme fills with unreasoning and childish laughter. Scold me, brothers, for limping verses are shorn of their power to keep me awake.

My slim resources are diminishing. I can calculate the hour when everything will be gone. I eat my bread, being almost in haste to finish it that I may no longer see it melt away at each meal. I am surrendering to want like a coward; the struggle for food terrifies me.

Ah! how they lie who assert that poverty is the mother of talent! Let them count those whom despair has made illustrious and those whom it has slowly debased. When tears are caused by a heart wound, the wrinkles they dig are beautiful and noble; but when hunger makes them flow, when every night a baseness or a brutish task drys them, they furrow the face frightfully, without imparting to it the sad serenity of age.

No; since I am so poor that I may, perhaps, die to-morrow, I cannot work. When the closet was full I had great courage. I felt the strength to gain my bread. Now it is nearly empty and I am given over to lassitude. It would be easier for me to endure hunger than to make the smallest effort.

I well know that I am cowardly and false to my vows. I know that I have not the right already to take refuge in defeat. I am only twenty: I cannot be weary of a world of which I am ignorant. Yesterday, I dreamed of it as sweet and good. Is it a new dream which makes me form a bad opinion of it to-day?

Oh! brothers, my first step has been unfortunate: I am afraid to advance. I will exhaust my suffering, shed all my tears, and my smiles will return. I will work with a gayer heart to-morrow.

ÉMILE ZOLA

VII

Laurence

Yesterday afternoon, I went to bed at five o'clock, in broad day, forgetting the key in the lock.

About midnight, as I saw in a dream a young blonde stretch out her arms to me, a sound which I had heard in my sleep made me suddenly open my eyes. My lamp was lighted. A woman, standing at the foot of the bed, was looking at me. Her back was towards the light, and I thought, in the confusion of awaking, that God had taken pity on me and transformed one of my visions into reality.

The woman approached. I recognized Laurence—Laurence with bare head, wearing her handsome blue silk dress. Her uncovered shoulders were purple with cold. Laurence had come to me.

"My friend," said she, "I owe the landlord forty francs. He has just refused me the key of my door and told me to seek shelter elsewhere. It was too late to go out, and I thought of you."

She sat down to unlace her boots. I did not understand, I did not wish to understand. It seemed to me that this girl had stolen into my garret to destroy me. The lamp, lighted I knew not how, the scantily-clad woman in the middle of the icy chamber, terrified me. I was tempted to shout for help.

"We will live as you like," continued Laurence. "I am not embarrassing."

I sat up to awaken myself completely. I began to understand, and what I understood was horrible. I restrained a harsh word which had arisen to my lips: abuse is repugnant to me, and I suffer when I insult any one.

"Madame," I simply said, "I am poor."

Laurence burst into a torrent of laughter.

"You call me Madame!" she resumed. "Are you angry? What have I done to you? I know you are poor—you showed me too much respect to be rich. Well, we will be poor."

"I can give you neither gewgaws nor enticing meals."

"Do you think that they have often been given to me? People are not so kind to poor girls! We roll in carriages only in novels. For one who finds a dress ten die of hunger."

"I eat but two very meagre meals a day; together, we could only have one, and that of bread dried that we might consume less of it, with simply water to drink."

"You wish to frighten me. Have you not a father, in Paris or elsewhere, who sends you books and clothes which you afterwards sell? We will eat your hard bread and go to the ball to drink champagne."

"No, I am alone in the world; I work for my living. I cannot associate you with my poverty."

Laurence stopped unlacing her boots. She sat still and thought.

"Listen," she said, suddenly: "I am without bread and without a shelter. You are young; you cannot conceive the extent of our perpetual distress, even amid luxury and gayety. The street is our sole domicile; elsewhere we are not at home. We are shown the door and we depart. Do you wish me to depart? You have the right to drive me away, and I the resource of going to sleep under some bridge."

"I do not wish to drive you away. I tell you only that you have ill-chosen your refuge. You can never accustom yourself to my sadness and want."

"Chosen! Ah! you think that we are permitted to choose! You may not believe it, but I came here because I knew not where else to go. I climbed the stairs furtively to pass the night upon a step. I leaned against your door, and then it was that I thought of you. You have only hard bread; I have not eaten anything since yesterday, and my smile is so faint that it will not bring me a meal to-morrow. You see that I can remain. I had just as well die here as in the street—besides, it is less cold."

"No; look further; you will find some one richer and gayer than I. Later you will thank me for not having received you."

Laurence arose. Her countenance had assumed an indescribable expression of bitterness and irony. Her look was not supplicating: it was insolent and cynical. She crossed her arms and stared me in the face.

"Come," said she, "be frank: you do not want me. I am too ugly, too miserable. I displease you, and you wish to get rid of me. You have no money, and yet you want a pretty sweetheart. I was a fool not to think of that. I ought to have said to myself that I was not worth even the attention of poverty and that I must descend a round of the ladder. I am thirsty, but I can drink from the gutters; I am hungry, but theft, perhaps, will afford me nourishment. I thank you for your advice."

She gathered her dress about her and walked towards the door.

"Do you know," hissed she, "that we wretches are better than you honest folks?"

And she talked for a long while in a sharp voice. I cannot reproduce the brutal force of her language. She said that she was the slave of our caprices, that she laughed when we told her to laugh, and that we turned our backs upon her later when we met her. Who forced us to seek her, who pushed us into her company in the darkness, that we should show so much contempt for her in broad day? I had once paid her a visit—why did I not want to see her now? Had I forgotten that she was a woman and as such was entitled even to my protection? The weak should always be protected and sheltered by the strong. Now that she was famished, I took a cruel delight in telling her that I had nothing for her to eat. Now that she was houseless, I gloried in telling her that I refused to give her a refuge. Because she was miserable I deemed it incumbent upon me to make her more miserable still, for the truth was that I could do so with impunity. I was afraid of her. She recalled the past too vividly. I wished to deny her very existence. I was, indeed, a man to be admired, a man with a noble, generous heart.

She was silent for an instant. Then she resumed, with more energy:

"You came to me and I received you as my husband. Now you deny that I have any rights. You lie. I have all the rights of a wife. You gave them to me, and you cannot undo what is done. You are mine and I am yours. You repudiate me and you are a coward!"

Laurence had opened the door. She hurled insults at me as she stood upon the threshold, pale with anger. I leaped from the bed and caught her by the arm.

"You can remain," I said. "You are like ice. Lie down, cover yourself up, and get warm."

Will you believe, brothers, that I was weeping! It was not pity. The tears flowed of themselves down my cheeks, though I felt only an immense and vague sadness.

The girl's words had made a deep impression on me. Her argument, the force of which, doubtless, escaped her, seemed to me just and true. I realized so perfectly that she had her rights, that I could not have driven her away without thinking myself the incarnation of injustice. She was a woman still, and I could not treat her like a lifeless object which contempt and abandonment cannot affect. Setting all else aside, humanity demanded that I should help her. The pure and the guilty are both liable to come to us, some winter night, to tell us that they are cold, that they are hungry, that they have need of us. Alas! we often receive the one and thrust the other into the gloomy and inhospitable street!

This is because we have the cowardice of our vices. It is because we would be terrified to have beside us a living remembrance and remorse. It pleases us to live honored, and when we blush at the call of some wretched creature, we deny her to explain our blushes by her impudence. And we do this without deeming ourselves culpable, without asking ourselves what justice this creature demands. Custom has made us consider her a disgrace, and we are astonished that this disgrace speaks and calls itself a woman.

My friends, I trembled before the truth. I understood and I wept. The question seemed to me simple, clear and self-evident. Laurence's words had frightened without disgusting me. I had not dreamed of her coming; but she came and I received her. I cannot, brothers, explain to you what were my feelings. My mind of twenty years had accepted in their absolute sense those words which admitted of no hesitation: "You are mine and I am yours!"

The next morning, when I awoke and found Laurence in my room, I felt my heart ready to burst with anguish. The scene of the past night was effaced. I no longer heard the true and rude words which had made me receive the girl. The brutal fact alone remained.

I looked at her as she slept. I saw her for the first time by daylight, without her face having the strange beauty of suffering or despair. When she thus appeared to me, ugly and prematurely old, plunged into a heavy, brutish slumber, I trembled before that faded and common countenance which I did not recognize. I could not comprehend how it was that I had awakened in such company. I seemed as if I had come out of a dream, and the reality proved so horrible that I had forgotten what had made me accept it.

But what difference did it make whether it was pity, justice or mercy. The girl was there. Ah! brothers, can I shed enough tears, and will you have sufficient courage to dry them!

VIII

A Mission from on High

Yes, I think as you do; I wish still to hope, I wish to make this fatal union a source of noble aspirations.

Formerly, when our thoughts drifted towards such unfortunate creatures as Laurence, we felt only mercy and pity for them. We discerned the holy task of redemption. We asked God to send us a dead soul, that we might, by kindly and gentle ways, restore it to youth and purity.

The faith of our sixteenth year, we thought, ought to make sinners believe and bow the head.

Then, we were Didier, pardoning Marion and acknowledging her as a wife at the foot of the scaffold. We lifted the sinner to the height of our tenderness.

Well, now I can be Didier. Marion, as sinful as the day he pardoned her, is here. She needs the white robe of purity, a hand to guide her wavering steps aright, to steady her in the narrow and difficult path which leads to the happiness of innocence. Her pale face requires a pure atmosphere to restore to it the glow of youthful health. What we wished for in our sainted hallucinations I have found without searching for it.

Since Laurence has come to me, I wish to erase all the evil instincts of her heart, to give it the healthful tone and freshness of mine. I will be a priest for this poor wretch: I will lift her up, console and pardon her.

Who knows, brothers, but that this is a supreme trial, an appointed task, that God has sent me! Perhaps, it is His wish, in charging me with a soul, to develop all the latent strength of mine. Perhaps, He has reserved for me the office of the strong, and does not fear to entrust me with the reformation of a human being. I will be worthy of His choice.

IX

The Course of Reformation

I desire to make Laurence forget what she is, to deceive her in regard to herself by the genuine friendship I show her. I speak to her only with gentleness; my words are always grave and carefully chosen.

Whenever she utters any of the slang of the street, I feign not to hear her. I inculcate the lessons of innocence, and treat her as a sister who has need of instruction. I oppose a calm and thoughtful life to her noisy life of the past. I pretend to ignore that this existence is not hers; I endeavor to be so natural in the imposition that, in the end, she will doubt that she ever lived otherwise.

Yesterday, in the street, a man insulted her. She was about to return insult for insult. I did not give her time. I approached the man, who was intoxicated, and caught him by the wrist, commanding him to respect my wife.

"Your wife!" cried he, ironically. "I know all about such wives!"

Then, I shook him violently, repeating my order in a sterner tone. He stammered out something and slunk away, begging pardon. Laurence silently resumed my arm, apparently confused by the title of wife which I had bestowed upon her.

I well know that too much austerity is not advisable. I do not hope for a sudden return to good; I wish to manage a skilful and gradual transition, which shall prevent her poor, sick eyes from being wounded by the light. There lies the whole difficulty of the task.

I have noticed that such girls as Laurence, women before their time, long keep the thoughtlessness and childishness of the infant. They are wearied and would yet willingly play with the doll. A trifle amuses them, makes them burst out laughing; they find again, unconsciously, the astonishment and caressing babble of little girls of five. I have taken advantage of this observation. I give Laurence gewgaws which make us great friends for an hour.

You cannot imagine the deep emotion this strange education has awakened in me. When I think I have made Laurence's dead heart beat, I am tempted to kneel and thank God. Without doubt, I exaggerate the sanctity of my mission. I say to myself that the love of a pure creature would sanctify me less than the devotion this poor girl will some day feel for me.

That day is yet afar off. My companion is embarrassed by my respect for her. She, whom insults do not affect, colors to the roots of her hair when I talk to her in a brotherly fashion, intent upon my good work. Sometimes, I see her hesitate before answering me, apparently doubting that it was to her I had spoken. She is amazed at not being reproached, and seems ill at ease because of my delicate attentions. The mask of innocence, which I have forced her to put on, worries her: she knows not how to bear esteem. Often I surprise a smile on her lips; she must think that I am mocking her, and this smile seems to ask me to kindly stop joking.

In the evening, at bed-time, she puts out the candle before undressing; she draws over her the corners of the coverings, and takes advantage of my sleep to leap from her couch in the morning. When she talks, she selects her words; following my example, she avoids being familiar with me.

I cannot tell why these precautions disturb me: I see in them more of constraint than true repentance. I feel that she acts and talks as she does out of fear of displeasing me, but that, so far as she herself is concerned, she is indifferent about her behavior and would as soon talk the language of the markets as not. She cannot have acquired so quickly a knowledge of her errors. I tell you, brothers, Laurence is afraid of me: such is the result of a week of respect.

As soon as she rises, she makes a grand toilet; she runs to the looking-glass and forgets herself there for an hour. She is in haste to repair the disorders of the night. Her thin locks are let fall, showing bare places on her head; her cheeks, from which the rouge has been rubbed, are pale and faded. She knows that she no longer has her borrowed youth, and is afraid that I will notice its absence should I turn my gaze upon her. The poor girl, who has lived beneath a coat of paint, fears lest I should drive her away when I see her without it. She combs her hair laboriously, puffing out her locks and skilfully concealing the vacant spots left by those which are gone; she blackens her eyelashes, whitens her shoulders and reddens her lips. Meanwhile I keep my back turned towards her, feigning to see nothing of all this. Then, when she has painted her face and thinks herself sufficiently young and beautiful, she comes to me smilingly. She is calmer, feeling certain that she is safe. She offers herself fearlessly to my eyes. She forgets that I cannot be deceived by the pretty colors she has put on, and seems to think that when I see them I am satisfied.

I told her in plain words that I preferred fresh water to pomades and cosmetics. I even went so far as to add that I liked her premature wrinkles better than the greasy and shining mask she put on her countenance every day. She did not understand. She blushed, thinking that I was reproaching her with her ugliness, and since then she has made increased efforts not to look like herself.

Thus combed and rouged, wrapped in her blue silk dress, she drags herself from chair to chair, careless and wearied. Not daring to stir for fear of deranging a fold of her skirt, she generally remains seated the rest of the day. She crosses her hands, and, with her eyes open, falls into a sort of waking sleep. Sometimes, she rises and walks to the window; there she leans her forehead against the icy panes and resumes her doze.

She was active enough before she became my companion. The agitated life she then led gave her a feverish ardor; her idleness was noisy and joyfully accepted the rude tasks set for it. Now, sharing my calm and studious existence, she has all the laziness of peace without its gentle and regular work.

I must, before everything else, cure her of carelessness and weariness. I plainly see that she regrets the strife, confusion and excitement of her early days, but she is by nature so devoid of energy that she is afraid to regret them openly. I have told you, brothers, that she fears me. She does not fear my anger, but she stands in terror of the unknown being whom she cannot comprehend. She vaguely seizes my wishes and bows before them, ignorant of their true meaning. Hence she is circumspect in her conduct without being repentant, and remains serious and tranquil without ceasing to be idle and lazy. Hence also she thinks that she cannot refuse my esteem, and, though she is sometimes amazed at it, she never seeks to be worthy of it.

X

THE EMBROIDERY STRIP

I suffered to see Laurence weighed down and languishing. I thought that toil was the great agent of redemption, and that the calm joy at the accomplishment of a task would make her forget the past. While the needle flies nimbly the heart awakes; the activity of the fingers gives to reverie a gayer and purer vivacity. A woman bent over her work has I know not what perfume of honesty. She is at peace and makes haste. Yesterday, perhaps, an erring creature, the workwoman of to-day has found again the active serenity of the innocent. Speak to her heart, it will answer you.

Laurence said she would like to be a seamstress. I desired that she should remain under my care, away from the workrooms. It seemed to me that quiet hours passed together, I inventing some story or other and she mingling her dream with the thread of her embroidery, would unite us in a gentler and deeper friendship. She accepted this idea of work as she accepts each one of my wishes, with a passive obedience, a singular mixture of indifference and resignation.

After considerable search, I discovered an aged lady who was willing to trust her with a bit of work to judge of her skill. She toiled until midnight, for I was to take home the work on the following morning. I watched her as she sewed. She seemed to be asleep; her sad expression had not left her. The needle, moving mechanically and regularly, told me that her body alone was working, her mind taking no part in the task.

The old lady pronounced the muslin badly embroidered; she declared to me that it was the work of a poor embroiderer, and that I never could find any one who would be satisfied with such long stitches and so little grace. I had feared this. The poor girl, having possessed jewels at fifteen, could not have had much experience with the needle. Fortunately, I sought in her work the slow cure of her heart, and not the skill of her fingers or the profit of her toil. In order not to give her back to idleness by imposing upon her a task myself, I resolved to hide from her the discouraging refusal of the old lady to employ her further.

I bought a stamped embroidery strip as I walked home. On entering, I told her that her work had given satisfaction and that she had been entrusted with more. Then, I handed her the few sous I had left, telling her I had received them as her pay. I knew that on the morrow, perhaps, I could not repeat this, and I regretted it. I desired to make her love the savor of bread honestly earned.

Laurence took the money without disturbing herself about the evening meal. She hastened away to purchase a row of velvet-covered buttons for her blue dress, which was already torn and stained. Never had I seen her so active; a quarter of an hour sufficed for her to sew on these buttons. She made a grand toilet, then admired herself. When night came on, she was still walking back and forth in the chamber, looking at her new buttons. As I lighted the lamp, I told her gently to go to work. She did not seem to understand me. I repeated my words, and then she sat down roughly, angrily seizing the embroidery strip. My heart was filled with sorrow.

"Laurence," said I, "it is not my wish to force you to work; put aside your needle, if you feel inclined to do nothing. I have not the right to impose a task upon you. You are free to be good or bad."

"No, no," she replied, "you want me to toil like a slave. I understand that I must pay for my food and my share of the rent. I might even pay your part, too, by working later at night."

"Laurence!" cried I, sadly. "Go, poor girl, and be happy. You shall not touch a needle again. Give me that embroidery strip."

And I threw the muslin into the fire. I saw it burn, regretting my hastiness. I had been unable to control my anguish, and was overwhelmed at the thought that Laurence was escaping from me. I had restored her to idleness. I trembled as I thought of the outrageous accusation she had made against me—that I wanted the money she might earn; I realized that it was no longer possible for me to advise her to work. So, it was all over; a single outburst on her part had sufficed to make me withdraw from her the means of redemption.

Laurence was not in the least surprised at my sudden rage. I have told you that she more readily accepts anger than affection. She even smiled at conquering what she called my weariness. Then she crossed her hands, happy in her idleness.

As I stirred the warm cinders on the hearth, I sadly asked myself what word, what sentiment, could awaken her stupefied soul! I was horror-stricken that I had not yet been able to restore to her the innocence of her childhood. I would have preferred her ignorant, eager to know. I was filled with despair at this sad indifference, this night satisfied with

ÉMILE ZOLA

its gloom, and so dense that it refused to admit the light. Vainly had I knocked at Laurence's heart: no answer had been returned to me. I was tempted to believe that death had passed over it and had dried up all its fibres. But a single quiver and I should have thought the girl saved.

But what was to be done with this nothingness, this desolated creature, this insensible marble which affection could not animate? Statues frighten me: they stare without seeing and have no intellect to understand.

Then, I said to myself that, perhaps, it was my fault if I could not make Laurence understand me. Didier loved Marion; he did not seek to save a soul—he simply loved—and yet he effected the miracle which my reason and kindness had sought in vain to accomplish. A heart awakes only at the voice of a heart. Love is the holy baptism which of itself, without the faith, without the science of good, remits every sin.

I do not love Laurence. That cold and wearied girl causes me only disgust.

Her voice and gestures seem insults in my eyes; her entire form wounds me. Deprived of every delicacy of mind, she makes the kindest word odious, and thrusts an outrage into each one of her smiles. In her everything becomes bad.

I strove to feign tenderness and approached her. She sat motionless, leaning towards the hearth, and allowed me to take her cold and inert hands. Then, I drew her near me. She lifted her head, questioning me with a look. Beneath that look I recoiled, repulsing her.

"Well, what do you want?" she asked.

What did I want! My lips were open to cry to her: "I want you to take off that wretched silk dress and put on honest calico. I want you to cease pining after your past career. I want you to listen to me and understand what I say. I want you to turn your thoughts towards innocence and goodness. I want to make you a worthy woman."

But, brothers, I did not say this. If I had loved her, I should without doubt have spoken, and, perhaps, she would have understood me.

XI

On the Way to the Ball

I think I have been lacking both in skill and prudence. I was in too great haste; I overshot the mark, without asking Laurence if she understood me. How can I, who am ignorant of life, teach its science? What means do I know how to employ, except the systems, the rules of conduct, dreamed of at sixteen, beautiful in theory, but absurd in practice? Is it enough for me to love the good, to stretch towards an ideal of virtue vague aspirations, the aim of which is itself uncertain? When reality is before me, I know how little these desires take practical shape, how powerless I am in the struggle it offers me. I shall never know how either to bind or conquer it, ignorant as I am of the way in which to seize it and unable even to avow to myself what victory I demand. A voice cries out in me that I do not want the truth, that I do not desire to change it, to transform what is evil in my sight into good. Let the world which exists stand; I have the audacity to wish to create a new land, without making use of the wrecks of the old. Hence, having no solid foundation, the scaffolding of my dreams crumbles at the slightest shock. I am only a useless thinker, a platonic lover of the good nursed by vain reveries, whose power vanishes as soon as he touches the earth.

Brothers, it would be easier for me to give Laurence wings than to give her a woman's heart.

We are but grown up children. We do not know what to do with that sublime reality, which comes to us from God and which we spoil at pleasure by our dreams. We are so awkward in living, that life, for this reason, becomes bad. Let us learn how to live and evil will disappear. If I possessed the great art of the real, if I had any conception of a human paradise, if I could distinguish the chimera from the possible, I could talk and Laurence would understand me. I would know how to take possession of her again and set her an example to follow. The delicate science which revealed to me the causes of her errors would find a remedy for each wound of her heart. But what can I do when my ignorance erects a barrier between her and me? I am the dream, she is the reality. We shall trudge on side by side without ever meeting, and, our journey finished, she will not have understood me, I will not have comprehended her.

I have decided to retrace my steps, in order to take Laurence such as she is and let her follow the road for which her human feet are fitted. I have resolved to study life with her, to descend that we may rise together. Since I am compelled to undertake this rough and disagreeable task, it is on the lowest step that I desire to start.

Would it not be a recompense great enough if I induced her to give me all the love of which she is capable? Brothers, I have a well grounded fear that our dreams are nothing but deceptions; I realize how weak and puerile they are in the presence of a reality of which I am vaguely conscious. There are days in which, further off than the sunlight and the perfumes, further off than those dim visions which I cannot turn to account, I catch a glimpse of the bold outlines of what is. And I comprehend that this is life, action and truth, while, in the surroundings which I have created for myself, move people strange to man, vain shadows whose eyes do not see me, whose lips cannot speak to me. The child can be pleased with these cold and mute friends; afraid of life, it takes refuge in that which does not live. But we men should not be satisfied with this eternal nothingness. Our arms are made for work.

Last night, as I was out walking with Laurence, we met a herd of maskers, packed into a carriage and going to the ball, intoxicated, in disorder, making a great noise. It is January, the most terrible of all the months. Poor Laurence was vastly moved by the cries of her kind. She smiled upon them, and turned that she might see them as long as possible. It was her former gayety which was passing by, her carelessness, her mad life so sharp that she could not forget its biting joys. She returned home sadder than ever and went to bed, sick of silence and solitude.

This morning, I sold some of my clothes and hired a costume for Laurence. I announced to her that we would go to the ball in the evening. She threw herself upon my neck; then, she took possession of the costume and forgot me. She examined each ribbon, each spangle; impatient to deck herself, she threw the soiled satin over her shoulders, intoxicating herself with the rustle of the stuff. Sometimes she turned, thanking me with a smile. I realized that she had never before loved me so much, and I could scarcely keep my hands from snatching the gewgaw which had brought me the esteem I had failed to acquire with all my kindness.

At last, I had made myself understood. I had ceased to be an unknown being in her eyes, a frightful compound of austerity and weariness. I was going to the ball like all the rest; like them, I hired costumes and amused my friends. I was a charming fellow and, like everybody else, loved buxom shoulders, cries and oaths. Ah! what joy! My wisdom was a sham!

Laurence felt herself in a country with which she was acquainted; she was no longer afraid; she had resumed her freedom of manner and gave vent to bursts of hearty laughter. Her familiar words, her easy gestures, filled her with satisfaction. She was perfectly at home in her present atmosphere.

This was what I wished, but I had hoped that a month of tranquillity, even though it had not succeeded in reforming her, had at least led her to forget somewhat her former ways. I had imagined that, when the mask fell, the face it would disclose would have less pallor about the lips and more blushes upon the cheeks. I was mistaken. The mask fallen, I had before me the same faded features, the same thick and noisy laugh. As this woman was when she entered my mansarde, rough, vulgar and cynical, so I again found her, after I had for a month protested against the infamy of her past life, silently to be sure, but every day. She had learned nothing, she had forgotten nothing. If her eyes shone with a new expression, it was only because of the miserable joy she felt on seeing that I seemed, at last, to have come down to her level. In view of this strange result, I asked myself if it would not be simply a waste of time to try again. I had wished for a real Laurence, and this Laurence, through whom ran a breath of life, terrified me more, perhaps, than the mournful creature of the past month. But the struggle promised to be so sharp that I heard, in the depths of my being, my audacity of twenty revolt at my repugnance and my fright.

As six o'clock struck, although the ball would not begin until midnight, Laurence began to make her toilet. Soon the chamber was in complete disorder: water, splashing from the wash-basin and dripping from the wet towels, flooded the floor; soap lather, fallen from Laurence's hands, spread out upon the planks in whitish patches; the comb was on the floor near the hair brush, and various articles of clothing, forgotten upon the chairs, on the mantelpiece and in the corners, were soaking amid pools of water. Laurence, to be more at her ease, had squatted down. She was washing herself energetically, throwing handfuls of water in her face and upon her shoulders. Despite this deluge, the soap, covered with dust, left broad streaks of dirt on her skin. At this she was in despair. Finally, she emptied the entire contents of the wash-basin over her.

Then she arose, shivering, her shoulders red, and began to use the towel.

The key had remained in the lock of the door. As Laurence was rubbing her neck with the icy towel, Pâquerette came in. The old woman visited us occasionally to get a stick or two from the hearth with which to kindle her fire, and pity prevented me from driving her off in disgust.

"Ah! my dear," cried Laurence to her, "come and help me a little. I'm tired of this wretched rubbing."

Pâquerette took the towel, and began to rub with all the strength of her wasted arms. She did not seem astonished at either the disorder of the chamber or Laurence's wholesale preparations for the ball. She quietly passed her stiff hands over the girl's fresh looking shoulders, envying their whiteness, thinking of the pleasures of the past. Laurence, her head half turned around, smiled upon her and shivered by fits.

"Where are you going, my child?" at last asked the horrible old woman.

"Claude has invited me to go to the ball."

"Ah! that's as it should be, Monsieur," resumed Pâquerette, ceasing to ply the towel and turning towards me.

Then, taking up a dry towel, she continued, as she affectionately wiped Laurence's arms:

"I said to myself only this morning that you would soon die of sadness, if you persisted in always remaining shut up in this chamber. Laurence is a good girl, Monsieur, a very good girl and a kind-hearted and indulgent one into the bargain. I know more than one such who would have quitted you twenty times, if subjected to the same treatment that Laurence has undergone for the past month. She is a miracle of patience and devotion to have remained. There, my child, you are as dry as a bone and as beautiful as a butterfly. You will have hosts of handsome and attentive gallants at the ball to-night! Are you jealous, Claude?"

I could not answer her. I smiled mechanically, and continued to gaze upon the strange scene. A single engrossing recollection, which unceasingly presented itself to my mind, prevented me from hearing what the old woman said. It was that of an antiquated engraving, which I had seen I know not where, representing Venus at her toilet, bathed by nymphs, caressed by little Cupids. The goddess has abandoned herself to the arms of her women, as young and beautiful as herself; the foam of the waves partially covers them, and, on the shore, an old faun stands lost in mute admiration and astonishment at the sight of so much youth and freshness.

"He is jealous, he is jealous!" cried Pâquerette, with a sharp laugh, broken by hiccoughs. "So much the better for you, my girl; he will make you more presents and it will be much easier for you to fool him. I once had an admirer, who strongly resembled you, Monsieur. He was a trifle shorter, I think, but he had the same eyes, the same mouth; he even wore his hair combed back, as you do. He adored me, overwhelmed me with attention and followed me everywhere, but, nevertheless, I dismissed him at the end of a week."

While Pâquerette was chattering, Laurence had dressed herself. She combed her hair, standing before the looking-glass, serious and thoughtful. The old woman stood beside her, as straight as a lance; she had ceased to babble, and was enviously contemplating the packages of rouge, and the vials of aromatic oils, common perfumery bought at a low price at stands in the open air. The two women having forgotten me, I sat down in a corner.

I saw their images in the looking-glass. Both the faces, despite the wrinkles of the one and the relative freshness of the other, seemed to me to have the same expression of degradation and baseness. The same looks stamped with dissipation, the same pale lips, were common to each. One could hardly read upon their faded cheeks the number of years which separated their ages. They were equally old in sin. For an instant I thought that I was endeavoring to reform Pâquerette instead of Laurence, and I closed my eyes to banish her from my sight.

They had forgotten that I existed. Occasionally they spoke in whispers. Laurence swore, striking her foot violently on the floor, when one of her rebellious locks refused to curl. Then the old woman spoke of her own flaxen tresses of other days; she described the style of coiffure of the girls of her time, and, to make herself better understood, arranged in her turn her gray locks before the looking-glass. Then followed long eulogies upon my companion's youth, endless lamentations in regard to the weariness of old age. Pâquerette said that her wrinkles had come to her long before she was ready for them, and that she greatly regretted not having enjoyed herself more when she was twenty. Now, she must live slowly in silence and gloom, having at heart a jealous admiration for those who could yet grow old.

ÉMILE ZOLA

Laurence listened, but only asked questions, demanding if such and such a curl became her, seeking for new praises. Then, when her locks, so long toiled over, had been satisfactorily arranged, her face was to be painted. Pâquerette wished to put the finishing touch to the masterpiece. She took red and blue pigments upon little balls of wadding, and passed them along the cheeks and around the eyes of the young woman. She enlarged her eyelids, purified her forehead and gave health to her lips. And, like us, poor dreamers, who daub reality with discordant colors and afterwards cry out that we have made a creation, she was amazed at her work, without seeing that her trembling hand had confused the features, exaggerated the red of the lips and made the eyelids too large. Beneath her fingers Laurence's visage had horribly changed, I thought. It had acquired in spots dull and earthy tints, while in other spots, which had been rubbed with ointment put on to fix the rouge, it shone with tremendous brilliancy. The stretched and irritated skin grimaced; the entire face, at once red and faded, had the silly smile of pasteboard dolls. The tones were so loud and so false that they wounded the sight.

Laurence, straight and motionless, her glance partially turned towards the looking-glass, complacently allowed herself to be rejuvenated. She scratched off with her finger-nail the touches which seemed to her too prominent. Leaning forward, she gravely studied for several seconds each of the beauties which Pâquerette gave her.

The work finished, the old woman drew back a few paces the better to scrutinize what she had done and note its effect. Then, satisfied, she exclaimed:

"Ah! my child, you look like a girl of fifteen!"

Laurence smiled contentedly. Both of these creatures were sincere; they frankly admired, not doubting in the least that a miracle had been worked. Then, they remembered me. Laurence, proud of the restored charms of her fifteenth year, came to embrace me, wishing to dazzle my eyes with her newly-acquired beauty. Her bare shoulders had the fresh and peculiar odor of a person who has just come out of a bath. At the touch of her cold lips, damp with rouge, I shivered with disgust.

"Bear me in mind, my child," said Pâquerette, as she was leaving the room. "Old women like sweetmeats."

We had yet two full hours to wait. I have no remembrance of any weariness so terrible. This waiting for a pleasure which clashed with all my tastes was indescribably uncomfortable and sad, and Laurence's impatience retarded still more for me the slow march of the minutes.

She was seated upon the bed, in her costume of pink satin ornamented with gilt spangles; this tinsel had the strangest effect in the world, brought into bold relief by the smoky paper on the chamber walls. The lamp burned dimly, the silence was broken only by the dashing of the rain against the window panes. Brothers, I do not know what demon then took possession of me, but I must admit to you, who know all my thoughts and feelings, that, sitting in the presence of that woman, abandoned by my cherished ideas, I caught myself wishing Laurence young and beautiful; I desired the power to transform my miserable mansarde into a delicious and mysterious retreat, a veritable nest for ideal happiness, with every surrounding of luxury and magnificence. For the moment, I lost all higher aspirations. What disgusted me was no longer vice, but ugliness and poverty.

At last, I went for a carriage and we started for the ball. Despite the lateness of the hour, the streets were still full of noise and light. Bursts of laughter came from every corner, groups of drunkards and women were in each drinking house. Nothing could be more odious to see than the people running in the mud, and elbowing each other amid the refrains of bacchanalian songs. Laurence, leaning out of the carriage window, laughed heartily at this disgusting joy. She called to the passers-by, seeking insult, happy at being able to participate in a war of rough words. As I remained mute, she said to me:

"Well! what on earth are you doing? Do you intend to go to sleep while you are taking me to the ball?"

I leaned out of the window in my turn; I sought for some one to insult. I would willingly have struck one of those brutes who were amused by such a spectacle as I then saw. Before me, upon the sidewalk, stood a tall young man with his shirt unbuttoned at the throat; a circle of laughers surrounded him, applauding each one of the many oaths he uttered. I shook my fist menacingly at him, for I was terribly exasperated. I hurled at him, as we went along, the most offensive epithets I could summon up.

"And your wife!" cried he, in reply. "Put her out here a little while, that we may pay her our compliments!"

The rough words of this man changed my anger into an indescribable sadness. I closed the window and leaned my forehead against the damp glass, leaving Laurence to her wretched pleasure. I was, so to speak, rocked by the cries of the crowd and the hollow roll of the vehicle. I saw, with the vague sight of a dream, the passers flee

ÉMILE ZOLA

behind me, strange shadows which lengthened and vanished without presenting any meaning to my mind. And, in this din, in this quick succession of darkness and light, I remember that I forgot everything for an instant, and gazed dreamily into the pools of water and mud between the pavements, upon which the lamps of the shops cast rapid reflections.

It was thus that we reached the ball-room.

To-morrow, brothers, I will tell you the rest. I cannot write everything now.

XII

The Public Ball

Oh! my remembrances, faithful companions, I cannot take a step in this world but you rise before me! When, with Laurence on my arm, I cast from a gallery a rapid glance around the ball-room full of noise and light, I saw again, in a sudden and sad vision, the smooth, stone-paved floor upon which the girls of Provence dance, in the evening, to the music of the fife and tambourine! How we used to ridicule them! The peasant girls, not those of our dreams, those who had the faces and the hearts of queens, but poor creatures whom the ardent soil had faded before their time, seemed to us to bound heavily, casting us silly smiles as they lumbered by. We closed our eyes against reality. We saw, beyond the horizon, immense palaces, halls paved with marble, with lofty and gilded roofs, filled with a whole nation of young women, who danced with the utmost harmony, in a cloud of lace spangled with diamonds. Truly, we were foolish children. Now, brothers, the peasant girls have taken vengeance for our disdain.

I beheld, from the gallery in which I found myself, a sort of oblong hall, of quite large dimensions, ornamented with faded paintings and gilding. A fine dust, raised by the dancers' feet, ascended slowly from the floor, like a mist, and filled the place. The bright flames of the gas looked red in this cloud; everything had a vague appearance, a strange hue of old copper. At the further end of the hall, galloped a frightful circle of creatures who could not be seen distinctly; the fury of their movements seemed to communicate itself to the thick and nauseous air; in the whirl, I thought I saw the walls tremble and turn with the crowd. A piercing clamor, accompanied by a sort of prolonged roll, drowned the music of the orchestra.

I cannot describe to you the first impressions produced on me by this place, in which each thing had in my eyes a special and unknown life. The shrill noises, the sonorous laughter bursting out like sobs, the frightful contortions of the furious dancers, the biting and suffocating odors, all came to me in a sharp sensation which filled my being with a vague terror, with which was mingled a sad pleasure. I could not laugh, for I felt my throat close, and yet I was unable to turn away my head, so delirious was the joy I experienced amid my suffering. I now understand the fascination of these exciting soirées. At the first sight one trembles, one refuses to lend himself to the terrible gayety; then intoxication comes, and, with bewildered brain, one abandons himself to the gulf. Common souls are soon won over. Those who have the strength of their dreams—dare I, brothers, count myself among them?—revolt, and, in their frankness, regret the humble dancing-floors of Provence upon which the awkward and lumbering peasant girls dance in the fresh, clear night.

From the gallery in which we were, we could see only the general effect of the scene. We quitted it, descending the stairways and reaching the main floor by passing through narrow and dark passages. Arrived in the ball-room, we were forced to follow a slender path contrived between the walls and the quadrilles. All my pleasure was gone; I now felt only disgust. The women were clad in tatters, in ragged silks spangled with dirty brass; their bare shoulders were dripping with perspiration; paint, in broad pools, in long streaks, reddened and blued their skin. One of them, with an inflamed visage and a hoarse voice, turned towards me, gesticulating and shouting. What a strange, hideous face she had! I shall see it again in my bad dreams!

I do not remember having noticed the men. They were, it seems to me, for the most part, standing straight and motionless, looking with great calmness at the tumultuous bounds of the women. I cannot tell you what kind of people they were, or if they appeared to comprehend the extent of their idiocy.

Weary already, feeling my head ready to split, I reached a table, dragging Laurence after me. We sat down, and I drank what the waiter brought me, studying my companion.

Laurence, at her entrance, had smiled, quivering with enjoyment, breathing her fill of that vitiated air so sweet to her lips. Her smile soon vanished and her countenance resumed its mournful look. Sometimes, she put out her arm and touched the hand of a woman or a man who passed. On such occasions her smile reappeared for a few seconds, and then vanished again. Partially thrown back upon her chair, her feet resting on a small bench, she rocked herself slowly, gazing into the ball-room with an air at once attentive and wearied. She looked from group to group in silence, turning her head at each new noise, seeming to wish to let nothing escape her. But there was so much fatigue in her attention that I asked myself, as I saw her pale and desolate face, what singular pleasure she could be experiencing to show so little of it.

Twice, thinking that my presence was a clog to her, I told her to leave me if she liked, to mingle with and greet her friends, to dance in perfect freedom.

"Why should I get up?" she tranquilly answered me. "I am very comfortable and perfectly satisfied. Are you weary of having me beside you?"

It was thus that we passed five hours, face to face, in a corner of the ball-room, I unconsciously sketching men's figures on the marble top of the table with a few drops of liquor spilled from a decanter, she maintaining despairing gravity and silence, her hands crossed upon her lap. I no longer had the least comprehension of what was going on around me. As the ball was drawing towards its close, I felt more like suffocating than ever. This was the last sensation that I remember having experienced. When the final galop drew me from this species of deep stupor, I saw Laurence arise; she swore and kicked aside the little bench, which had become entangled among her skirts; then, she took my arm, and we made a final tour of the ball-room before departing. Upon the threshold, Laurence turned with a yawn, casting a last look at the disordered circle of dancers who were vociferating in the midst of a frightful din.

When we reached the street, an icy blast, which struck me in the face, gave me a delicious feeling. I felt that I was restored to the good, to free and energetic life; the intoxication which had possessed me was driven away, and, beneath the drizzling winter rain, I had an instant of ineffable pleasure, casting from me all the disgusts of the mad night. I comprehended the wretchedness I had left behind me; I would have preferred to go home on foot through the streets, allowing the glacial water to penetrate me and renew my being.

Laurence shivered at my side. She had fastened her handkerchief over her bare shoulders; not daring to venture on, she looked in a despairing way at the sombre sky and at the gutters which were overflowing upon the pavements. The poor girl thought the wintry sky capable only of giving her inflammation of the lungs.

I had two francs left. I hailed a fiacre and helped Laurence into it. She gathered herself up in one of the corners and there sat silently, without ceasing to shiver. I saw her on my left, like a patch of tarnished white. Sometimes, a drop of water, which had remained upon her garments, rolled as far as my hand.

After an instant had elapsed, a sort of drowsiness seized upon me and sleep closed my eyes. As I dozed, I seemed to hear the din of the

ÉMILE ZOLA

ball; the jolts of the vehicle whirled me away as in a furious dance, and the axle-trees, with their sharp noise, played those airs which all night long had filled my ears. When, feverish and excited, I opened my eyes, I stared stupidly at the sides of the narrow box which seemed to me full of music and tumult. Then, I felt a biting sensation of cold; finding beneath my hand the icy hand of Laurence, I remembered where I had been and realized where I was. Without, the rain was still falling; the flickering lights fled rapidly behind us.

Fatigue once more made me close my eyes, and again I was drawn into the midst of gigantic circles of dancers, incessantly renewed. It seems to me now that I remember vaguely having danced thus for long hours. I found myself nailed to a bench, beside a shivering woman, and I whirled I know not how in a sort of box which rolled with a tremendous noise at the bottom of a glacial gulf.

Having ascended to my chamber, while Laurence was taking off her costume, I threw all my remaining wood upon the fire, which was faintly burning upon the hearth. Then, I hastened to bed, happy as a child to find myself again amid my poverty, gazing with loving glances at the broad lights and shadows which the flames of the hearth caused to dance up and down along my poor walls. Calmness had taken possession of me from the moment I crossed the threshold of this retired chamber. With my head upon the pillow, at peace and almost smiling, I gazed at my companion who, standing pensively before the fire, was removing her garments one by one.

She soon came to me, and sat down at my feet on the edge of the bed. Breaking, at last, the silence which she had maintained until then, she began to talk with extreme volubility.

Enveloped in an old wrapper, with her feet drawn up under her and her hands clasped in front of her knees, she indulged in loud bursts of laughter, throwing her head backwards. She seemed to be in haste to throw off all the words, all the gayety, she had amassed. For nearly a whole hour she entertained me with a recital of the thousand incidents of the ball. She had seen everything, heard everything. She gave vent to exclamations without end, sudden joys, hurried and tumultuous reminiscences. A man had slipped in such a way, a woman had sworn in such another way; Jeanne wore a milkmaid's costume which became her marvellously; Louise looked hideous as a Scotch lassie; as to Edouard, he had certainly pawned his watch that very morning. And she rattled on, always finding some new detail, repeating the same circumstance ten times rather than pause. Then, shivering with cold, she finally went to bed. She asserted that she had never before been so much amused at a ball, and made me promise to take her to another as soon as I possibly could. She fell asleep thus, while still talking to me, laughing amid her slumber.

This sudden awakening to life, this flood of feverish words, strangely astonished me. I could not then and I cannot now explain to myself the coldness and indolence of this girl amid the tumult of the night, and her bursts of gayety, her chatter of the morning in our sad and silent chamber. Why had she torn from me the promise to take her as soon and as often as possible to these balls, where she laughed so little and did not dance at all? Besides, if she were acting in good faith, what was that singular joy which had manifested itself by silence and ill-humor during the soirée, and, later, had broken out in thick and delighted laughter?

Oh! what an unknown world is that of the flesh and dissipation, in which I find food for amazement at every step! I dare not as yet critically examine all this wretchedness, the motives of this puzzling woman, cold in her feelings, weary and half asleep amid her joys! I took her to the ball to save her, but she had come back from it more terrible, more impenetrable than ever!

XIII

An Acceptance of Reality

You complain of my silence; you are uneasy, and ask me what new sorrows have made the pen fall from my fingers.

Brothers, my new sorrows are caused by the fact that our ridiculous fancies of childhood are being dissipated one by one. This adieu to early hopes has, in its salutary harshness, the most profound bitterness. I feel myself becoming a man; I weep over my departing weaknesses, taking, at the same time, a great pride in the strength I am acquiring.

Ah! how silly youth would be, if it had not its beautiful simplicity! The foolishness upon the lips of the child is an adorable ignorance by which men are quietly amused. Scarcely a month ago, I was a simpleton; I spoke to you innocently of the redemption of women. Verily, to have heard me, an old man would at once have smiled his sweetest smile and ironically shaken his head: he would have given the smile to the young soul who had faith in entire perfection, and addressed the shake of the head to the absurd youth who was boldly attempting the miracle which the Saviour alone has the power to work.

Enough of deceptions! The brutal truth has strange delights for those who are tormented by the problem of life; they are weary of those hopes which mothers bequeath to their children, and which, slow to vanish, abandon them one by one, lengthening their martyrdom. As for me, I prefer, even should I suffer from having all my illusions torn from me in a day, to see clearly into this world of dissipation to the depths of which I have descended.

No doubt, some once sinful women who have sincerely repented are met with. Women who have strayed from the right path have seen the error of their ways, have reformed, have found husbands and have been pardoned. But such things are miracles. The laws common to short-sighted humanity seem to ordain that wretched women, who have once forgotten themselves, shall be trodden under foot, torn to pieces, and their fragments so scattered that they cannot be reunited at the final hour.

Listen, brothers: should a Magdalen crawl at your feet, cursing her past errors, promising you a new youth of love, do not believe her.

Heaven is not lavish of prodigies. Providence rarely shackles human misfortunes. Say to yourselves that evil is powerful, and that in this world of ours falsehood is not changed into truth even to give relief to a poor, suffering soul. Repulse the Magdalen, spurn her, laugh at her tears and the pleading of her heart; rail against all redemption. Such is the advice of what men call wisdom.

I feel that I am gaining experience in worldly matters.

Laurence is a soul forever lost, a stupefied intelligence, a creature so hardened that nothing can awaken her from her sleep in the mud. I might bruise her flesh, I might break her bones with a club, or I might lift her drowsy eyelids with kisses, but she would still squat at my feet, without a quiver, without a cry either of pain or joy. Sometimes, I am tempted to cry out to her:

"Get up and let us fight; awake, shout, swear, and show me that you are yet alive by making me suffer!"

She looks at me with her dull eyes; I recoil affrighted, not daring to speak. Laurence is dead, dead in heart and in thought. I can do nothing with such a corpse.

Brothers, I have no longer the slightest hope; I no longer wish to trouble myself about this girl. She has refused my life of toil and I cannot accept her life of dissipation. The dream was too lofty; the reality seems to me like a bottomless pit. I have paused and am waiting. For what? I do not know!

I have only to justify myself in your eyes. I know that you see clearly into my soul, that you explain my acts to yourselves by thoughts of justice and duty. You have more confidence in me than I myself dare to have. At times I question myself, I judge myself as I am, no doubt, judged by the passers whom I elbow in this life; I am afraid of the vice which surrounds without corrupting me, of the woman who remains in my presence without being my companion. Then, in utter despair, I am tempted to do what others would do, to take Laurence by the shoulders and push her back into the street from whence she came. Should I do this, she would resume her old career as madly, as recklessly, as ever, bearing upon her forehead the stamp of the same wretchedness and infamy as before. And I would calmly close my door, having stolen nothing from her, owing her nothing. Men's consciences are very elastic; there are people who possess the science of remaining honest by becoming cowardly and cruel.

Laurence has thrust herself upon my protection with all the strength of her abandonment. She remains with me, tranquil and passive. I cannot, however, drive her away. My poverty prevents me from paying her to go. We are fatally bound one to the other by misfortune. As long as she shall feel inclined to stay, I shall believe it my duty to accept her presence.

Hence I am waiting, and, I repeat, I know not for what I am waiting. Like Laurence, I am weighed down, I live in a sort of somnolence at once mild and sad, without suffering too greatly, feeling in my heart only a colossal fatigue. After all, I am not irritated against this girl; I feel more pity than anger, more sadness than hatred.

I no longer struggle, I abandon myself; I find in the certainty of evil a strange repose, a pacification of my entire being.

XIV

JACQUES AND MARIE

You remember tall Jacques, that long, pale and quiet lad, do you not? I see him yet, walking in the shade of the plane trees on the college green; he walked with a slow and firm step, kicking away the pebbles with his foot; he laughed tranquilly, was logical in his smiles and lived in supreme indifference. I remember that, on a day of effusion, he confided to me the secret of his strength. I understood nothing of his disclosures, except that he designed to live happily by ripening his heart and mind.

When fifteen, I dreamed only of tall Jacques. I envied his long blond hair, his superb indolence. He was, among us, a type of elegance and aristocratic disdain. I was surprised by his selfish nature, which had nothing either young or generous about it; I admired the dull and cold lad who went among us with the indulgent and superior gravity of a man.

I have seen tall Jacques again. He is my neighbor; he lives in the same house as I, two floors lower down. Yesterday, as I was mounting the stairway, I met a young man and a young woman who were descending. The young man, without hesitation and in the most natural manner in the world, extended me his hand.

"How are you, Claude?" he said to me.

He acted as if he had quitted me only the previous day. He had scarcely looked at my face, but I looked at his in the partial obscurity of the landing, without being able to recognize his features. His hand was cold. I know not by what strange sensation I recognized his calm and indifferent flesh.

"Is it you, Jacques?" I cried. "Good heavens! you are taller than ever!"

"Yes, yes, it is I," answered he, with a smile. "I lodge there, at the end of the passage, number 17. Come and see me this evening, between seven and eight o'clock."

And he went down-stairs, without turning his head, preceded by the young woman who stared at me with the wide open eyes of a child. I stood still for an instant, leaning over the railing, and looked after this youth who was departing with a calm step, while my heart was leaping violently in my breast.

In the evening, I went down to number 17. The chamber was fitted up with the false and discouraging luxury of the furnished lodging-houses of Paris. You cannot imagine, brothers, the wretched and shameful air of the frayed red hangings, gray with dust, of the dirty and greasy furniture, of the cracked faïences, of the nameless objects, rags and wrecks which were spread out along the damp walls. My mansarde is barer, but not so hideous. Two large and lofty windows, garnished with thin muslin curtains, threw a raw light over all this rubbish. One saw a wardrobe with glass doors, which was tarnished and had one side broken; a bed enveloped by faded curtains; a miserable sofa and deplorable arm-chairs, yellow from use; besides, the room contained a toilet-bureau, a desk, a table, chairs, odd pieces of furniture—furniture which had served in dining-rooms, bed-chambers, parlors and offices. The general effect had I know not what of pretentiousness and filth which disgusted me. At the first glance, one might think he had entered the chamber of the right sort of people; at the second, one saw the dirt on the mahogany and on the damask, and one felt that he was amid vice and slovenliness.

I was saddened by the unhealthful aspect of this chamber; I breathed with disgust the thick and nauseous air, smelling of dust, old varnish and faded stuffs, a biting and stifling odor which is common to all furnished lodging-houses.

Jacques, seated at the desk, was toiling away peacefully, a Code open before him. The young woman I had met on the stairway was lying upon the sofa, her eyes fixed on the ceiling, silent and grave.

Jacques half turned his chair; his face appeared to me in the full light. It was still the same visage of other days, a superb and indifferent visage; one read in it a strong will, made up of selfishness and coldness. The man had become what the boy promised to be. Our former comrade must be what the world calls a practical and serious person; he has an aim: he wishes to be a counselor, a lawyer or a notary, and moves onward towards his goal with all the power of his tranquillity. With closed heart and calm flesh, he accepts this world without either thanks or revolt. Jacques has an honest nature, a just mind; he will live honorably, according to duty and custom; he will not weaken, because he will not have to weaken; he will pass on, straight and firm, having nothing either to hate or to love. In his clear and empty eyes, I do not find the soul; upon his pale lips I do not see the blood of the heart.

In the presence of this quiet and smiling young man, bending over his law books and extending to me his cool hand, I thought of myself, brothers, of my poor being incessantly shaken by the fever of wishes and regrets. I advance staggeringly; I have not to protect me Jacques' imperturbable tranquillity, his silence of heart and of soul. I am all flesh, all love; I feel myself profoundly vibrate at the least sensation. Events lead me; I can neither conduct nor surmount them. To-morrow, in my free life, if I should happen to wound the world, the world will turn from me, because I obeyed my pride and my tenderness. Jacques will be saluted, having followed the common route. I dare not say aloud that virtue is a question of temperament; but, brothers, I think all the same that the Jacqueses upon this earth are basely virtuous, while the Claudes have the frightful misfortune of having in them an eternal tempest, an immense desire for the good, which agitates them and leads them beyond the judgment of the crowd.

The young woman had taken her glance from the ceiling and was looking at me, with partially open lips and curious eyes. Her face had the transparent whiteness of wax, with dull flushes on the cheeks; her pale lips, her soft and brown eyelids gave to her visage the air of a sick and resigned child. She was fifteen, and, at times, when she smiled, one would have thought her scarcely twelve.

While Jacques was talking to me in his slow voice, I could not take my eyes from the young girl's touching countenance, so youthful and so faded. There were upon her frank forehead profound lassitude and languor; the blood no longer flowed beneath her skin; the shivers of life no longer made her slumbering flesh tremble. Have you ever seen, in her cradle, a little girl whom fever has rendered whiter and more innocent than usual? She sleeps with her eyes wide open; she has the gentle and peaceful visage of an angel; she suffers and she seems to smile. The strange little girl whom I had before me, that woman who had remained a child, resembled her sister in the cradle. Only, in her case, it was more pitiful to see upon a forehead of fifteen so much purity and so much pallor, all the innocent graces of a young girl and all the shameful fatigues of a woman.

She had thrown back her arms and was supporting her languishing head upon her hands. I was ignorant of her history; I knew not who she was or what she was doing in this chamber. But, from her entire being, I saw the innocence of her heart and the disgrace of her life; I recognized the youthfulness of her glances and the premature age of her blood; I said to myself that she was dying of decrepitude at fifteen, with a spotless soul. Emaciated and weakened, she would expire like a fallen creature, but with the smile of an angel upon her lips.

I sat for two full hours between Jacques and Marie, contemplating these two beings, studying their countenances. I could not conjecture what had brought such a man and such a woman together. Then, I thought of Laurence, and comprehended that unions existed which could not be avoided.

Jacques seems to me satisfied with the existence he leads. He toils, he regulates his pleasures and his studies; he lives the life of a student without impatience, even with a certain tranquil satisfaction. I noticed that he showed some pride in receiving me in such a beautiful chamber; he does not see all the ignoble ugliness of the false and wretched luxury which surrounds him. Besides, he is neither vain nor a coxcomb; he is a great deal too practical to have such defects. He spoke to me only of his hopes, of his future position; he is in haste to be no longer young and to live as becomes a grave man. Meanwhile, in order to be like the rest of mankind, he consents to inhabit a chamber at fifty francs per month rent, he wishes to smoke, to drink a little, and even to have a sweetheart. But he considers all this simply as a custom which he cannot refuse; he designs, after having passed his final examination, to disembarrass himself of his cigar, of Marie and of his glass as pieces of furniture thenceforward useless. He has calculated, nearly to the minute, the time when he will have a right to the respect of worthy people.

Marie listened to Jacques' theories with perfect calmness. She did not appear to comprehend that she was one of those pieces of furniture which a young man would abandon on removing from one circle of society to another. The poor girl, doubtless, cares very little who protects her, provided that she has a sofa upon which she can rest her painful limbs.

Besides, Jacques and Marie talked together with a gentleness which surprised me. They seemed to accept each other, to take care of each other. There is not love, not even friendship in their discourse; it is a polite language which shuns every quarrel and keeps the heart in a state of complete indifference. Jacques must have been the inventor of this language.

After an hour had elapsed, Jacques declared that he could not afford to lose any more time; he resumed his work, begging me to remain, assuring me that my presence would not annoy him in any way whatever. I drew my chair up to the sofa, and chatted in a low voice with Marie. This woman attracted me; I felt for her all the tenderness and pity of a father.

She talked like a child, now in monosyllables, now with volubility, enthusiastically and without pausing. I had formed a correct opinion of her: her intelligence and heart have remained those of an infant, while, physically, she has grown up and strayed from the path which leads to true happiness. She is exquisitely innocent; horribly so sometimes, when, with a sweet smile upon her lips and large, astonished eyes, she allows rude words to escape from her delicate mouth. She does not blush, being totally ignorant of blushes; she does not seem to realize her condition, and is slowly dying, without knowing either what she is or what are the other young girls who turn away their heads when she passes them on the streets.

Little by little, she told me the story of her life. I was able, phrase by phrase, to reconstruct this lamentable story. A connected narrative would not have satisfied me, for I should have hesitated to believe. I preferred that she should make a confession, without knowing she was doing so, by partial avowals, in the course of conversation.

Marie thinks she is fifteen years old. She does not know where she was born, but vaguely remembers a woman who beat her, her mother without doubt. Her earliest recollections date from the streets; she recalls that she played there and that she slept there. In fact, her life has been a long walk in the thoroughfares. It would be very difficult for her to tell what she did up to the age of eight; when I questioned her in regard to her early years, she replied that she had forgotten all about them, except that she was very hungry and very cold. In her eighth year, like all the little outcasts, she sold flowers. She slept then at the Fontainebleau gate, in a large, gloomy garret which was the refuge of a whole herd of children of the same age as herself, all of whom had been abandoned by their parents to the cold charity of the world. Until she was fourteen, she went to this kennel, choosing her corner every night, sometimes well received by her companions, sometimes beaten by them, growing up amid wretchedness and want, nobody stretching out a hand to save her or uttering a word to awaken her heart. She was in the deepest ignorance, and did not even know that she possessed a mind and a soul. She acquired evil ways, without suspecting that evil existed; at present, though she had become a woman of the world, she still had her childish face and her mind was yet infantile and innocent. She had strayed too early in life for sin to touch her soul.

I now understood the meaning of her strange visage, made up of shamelessness and innocence, of beauty at once youthful and faded. I had the key to the mystery of this cynical girl, this weary woman, who was dying with the calmness and the whiteness of a martyr. She was the daughter of the great city, and the great city had made of her a monstrous creature neither a child nor a woman. In that being, whose soul no one had awakened, that soul still slumbered. The body itself had, doubtless, never been aroused. Marie was a creature simple in mind and flesh, who, while she had trodden muddy paths, had remained pure amid the mud, knowing nothing and accepting everything. I saw her before me, already branded, with her sweet smile, talking to me of herself, in her somewhat hoarse voice, as our little sisters talk to us of their dolls, and I felt a sickening sensation take possession of my heart.

When Marie reached fourteen, an old woman, who had no right whatever to her, sold her. She allowed herself to be bought; she almost offered herself for sale, as she had offered her bouquets of violets. She still had rosy cheeks, and her laughter rang out gayly. She now had silk dresses and jewels; she accepted the silk and the gold as she would have accepted playthings, tearing, wasting everything. But Marie lived thus, because she did not know that one could live in any other way; she could not appreciate the value of luxury, and would have accepted with indifference either a hovel or a hôtel. It pleased her to live in idleness, to look at the walls; suffering, which had already bent her, made her love repose, a sort of vague reverie, on coming out of which she seemed uneasy and agitated. When one interrogated her, asking her what she had seen, she responded in a bewildered tone: "I do not know!"

She lived thus for nearly a year, running about among the furnished lodging houses, sometimes living in one, sometimes in another, without losing anything of her serenity. As I showed some surprise and could not vanquish all the disgust with which such an existence filled me, she was greatly amazed and did not in the least understand my feelings.

One evening, poverty returned to her, and Marie was on her way back to the garret at the Fontainebleau gate, when she met Jacques. She told me of this meeting in a voice which I shall never forget, with a stony look in her eyes and noisy laughter upon her lips. It was she who spoke to Jacques, asking him for his arm because it was dark and the pavement was slippery. She had no other thought than to obtain his aid for the moment. Jacques questioned her, drew her story from her and took pity on her. He offered her a shelter more suitable for her than that to which she was going, and took her to the house in which he lived. She made no objection, maintaining her usual calmness. She would not, perhaps, have asked any one for a bed, for she had thought only of the straw in the garret at the Fontainebleau gate, but she accepted the feathers and white sheets, which had fallen from the sky, without either joy or repugnance. From that time, she had lived as much as possible on the sofa.

I can easily imagine that Jacques thought he had made a good acquisition, in offering his protection to Marie. She was in every way suited to become his companion. She was of a weak and calm nature, and would not trouble him in his indifference; she was a careless girl of whom he could easily disembarrass himself, a woman charming in her pallor, who had all the grace of youth without having either its caprices or its inconsistency. Besides, Marie, though sometimes suffering, has her days of life and gayety; she is not yet nailed to a mattress, and, when she laughs in the sunshine, among her flaxen curls, she glows with enough beauty to make Jacques himself dream.

It pleases me, brothers, to talk to you of Jacques and Marie.

I remained two or three hours with them, forgetting my sufferings, and I wished to forget them still longer in describing to you my visit. It will give you a glimpse of a world of which you are ignorant. That world is touching; the study of it is biting, full of vertigo. I would penetrate into its hearts and souls; I am attracted by these women and men who live around me. Perhaps, when I analyze them, I shall be discouraged at the result, but I love to analyze, nevertheless. These people live a life so strange, that I believe myself always to be upon the point of discovering in them new truths.

ÉMILE ZOLA

XV

BITING POVERTY

We eat from day to day, selling old books or a few old clothes to get money. My poverty is such that I no longer have any comprehension of it, and that I go to sleep at night almost satisfied when I have twenty sous remaining with which to purchase the two meals of the morrow.

I have been to many offices to solicit employment. I have always been received with roughness; I comprehend that I was guilty of the sin of being poorly clad. I wrote a bad hand, they said; I was good for nothing. I believed their words and retired, ashamed of having had, for an instant, the thought of robbing these honest people by putting my intelligence and will at their service.

I am good for nothing—such is the truth that I have learned by my attempts. I am good for nothing, except to suffer, to sob, to weep over my youth and my heart. Hence, behold me alone in the world, repulsed and miserable, not daring to beg, and feeling myself more famished than the poor wretch who holds out his hand for alms. I came to Paris, plunged in a dream of glory and fortune; I have awakened in the midst of mud and distress.

Happily, Heaven is kind and good. There is in want a sort of heavy intoxication, a pleasurable somnolence, which puts to sleep the conscience, the flesh and the mind. I do not clearly feel my degree of indigence and infamy; I suffer little from my destitution; I doze in my hunger and grovel in my idleness.

This is my life:

In the morning, I rise late. The mornings are foggy, cold and wan; the light enters, gray and sad, through the curtainless window; it lies about in a melancholy way upon the floor and walls. I experience a sensation of comfort in feeling the agreeable warmth of the garments I heap upon the bed. Laurence sleeps a sleep of lead, her face thrown back and expressionless. As for me, with open eyes, the covers drawn to my chin, I stare at the dingy ceiling which is crossed by a long chink. I fall into an ecstasy before this chink; I study it, I follow delightedly with my glance its broken lines; I contemplate it for hours at a time, without thinking of anything.

This is the best period of the day. I am warm and half asleep. My flesh is satisfied, my mind strays gently through that beautiful land of partial slumber in which life has all the pleasures of death. Then, sometimes, when I am completely awakened, I abandon myself to the sway of some dream. Brothers, what a child my poor heart must be that I can still lie to it! Ah! yes, I dream constantly, I yet have that strange power of escaping from reality, of creating from its wrecks a better world and better beings. There, between two dirty sheets, in the immediate vicinity of a woman hideous and wretched in her degradation, in the midst of a gloomy chamber, I often see a palace, all marble and silver, and a spotless, beautiful sweetheart, who stretches out her arms to me and summons me to quit my miserable retreat and its shameful surroundings.

Eleven o'clock strikes and I leap from bed. The damp cold of the floor, which suddenly chills the soles of my feet, draws me from my dream. I shiver and dress myself. Then I walk about the room, going from the window to the door, glancing at the wall which bounds my horizon, and returning to stare at Laurence without seeing her. I smoke, yawn and try to read. I am cold and weary.

Laurence awakes. Then begins the chapter of suffering. We must eat. We talk the matter over. We search the chamber for some object to sell. Often we give up the idea of breakfasting, when the problem is too difficult to solve and all is said. When we have happened to find some old rag, some piece of paper, no matter what, Laurence dresses herself and goes to offer the deplorable merchandise to a second-hand dealer, who gives her eight or ten sous. She brings back bread and a little pork which we eat as we stand, without talking to each other.

The days are long for the wretched. When it is too cold and we have no fire, I go to bed again. When the weather is milder I strive to toil, giving myself a fever in trying to carry on work which does not desire me any longer.

Laurence throws herself into a chair or walks about with slow steps. She drags along her blue silk dress, which seems to weep as it rustles past the furniture. This rag is all yellow with grease, all torn, ripped at the seams and worn at the folds. Laurence lets it get soiled and tattered, without either cleaning or mending it. She puts it on in the morning, having nothing else to wear, and walks in it the whole day about this miserable chamber, with dishevelled locks, the low-necked ball dress displaying her back and throat. And this dress, this soft silk of a pale blue color, which still shines in spots, is an infamous, twisted, faded and lamentable rag. I experience I know not what keen anguish on seeing these shreds of rich tissue, this luxury dragged about in the midst of want, this woman's bare shoulders reddened by the cold. I shall always remember Laurence walking about, thus clad, in the den sacred to my twentieth year.

In the evening, the question of bread returns, terrible and pressing. We eat or we do not eat. Then, we retire, weary and sleepy. On the morrow, the same life begins again, but sharper and more biting every day.

I have not been out of doors for a week past. One evening—we had not eaten the previous day—I took off my coat on the Place du Panthéon, and Laurence went to sell it. It was freezing. I went home on a run, sweating great beads from fear and suffering. Two days afterwards my pantaloons followed the coat. I no longer have clothes to wear. I wrap myself up in a coverlet, I cover myself as I can and take thus the most exercise possible to prevent my joints from stiffening. When any one comes to see me, I hurry to bed and pretend to be a trifle indisposed.

Laurence appears to suffer less than I do. She feels no shock, she does not try to escape from the existence we lead. I cannot comprehend this woman. She tranquilly accepts my poverty. Is it devotion or necessity?

As for me, brothers, as I have told you, I am comfortable, I am plunged in lethargy. I feel my being melting away; I abandon myself to that gentle prostration of dying men, who ask for pity in a weak and caressing tone. I have no desire whatever, except to eat more frequently. I would also be pitied, caressed and loved. I have need of a heart.

OH! BROTHERS, I SUFFER, I SUFFER. I dare not speak; I feel shame close my lips, and I can only weep, without taking from my breast the crushing weight which is upon it.

Poverty is mild and infamy light. And now Heaven is punishing me, bowing me beneath a terrible hurricane, beneath an implacable wound.

At last, brothers, you can give up all hope of me: I have no more steps to descend, for I am at the bottom of the ladder; I am about to abandon myself to the gulf—I am lost forever.

Do not question me. I allow my cries to float to your ears, for grief is too bitter for me to succeed in stifling its groans. But I restrain the words upon my lips; I wish neither to frighten you nor to sadden you with the recital of the terrible history of my heart.

Say to yourselves that Claude is dead, that you will never see him more, that all is, indeed, over. I prefer to suffer alone, even if I should die of my suffering, to troubling your holy tranquillity by tearing myself open before you, by showing you my bleeding wound.

No, you will suffer from the revelation, but it is impossible for me to maintain silence. I will find some consolation in imparting to you all my thoughts and actions; I will be quieted when I know that you are sobbing with me.

Brothers, I love Laurence!

XVI

Reminiscences

L et me regret, let me remember, let me review all my youth in a single glance.

We were then twelve years old. I met you one October evening upon the college green, beneath the plane trees, near the little fountain. You were weak and timid. I know not what united us; our weakness, perhaps. From that evening, we walked together, separating from each other for a few hours, but clasping hands with stronger friendship after each separation.

I know that we have neither the same flesh nor the same heart. You live and think differently from me, but you love as I do. There is the secret of our fraternity. You have my tenderness and my pity; you kneel in life, you seek some one upon whom to bestow your souls. We have a communion of tenderness and affection.

Do you remember the first years of our acquaintance? We read together idle tales, grand romances of adventure which held us for six months beneath their fascinating spell. We wrote verses and made chemical experiments; we indulged in painting and music. There was, at the house of one of us, on the fourth floor, a large chamber which served as our laboratory and atelier. There, in the solitude, we committed our childish crimes: we ate the raisins hanging from the ceiling, we risked our eyes over retorts brought to a white heat, we wrote rhymed comedies in three acts which I yet read to-day when I wish to smile. I still see that large chamber, with its broad window, flooded with white light and full of old newspapers, engravings trodden under foot, chairs with their straw bottoms gone, and broken wood horses. It seems to me pleasant and smiling, when I look at my chamber of to-day and perceive, standing in the middle of it, Laurence who terrifies and attracts me.

Later, the open air intoxicated us. We enjoyed the healthful dissipation of the fields and long walks. It was madness, fury. We broke the retorts, forgot the raisins and closed the door of the laboratory. In the morning, we set out before day. I came beneath your windows to summon you in the midst of darkness, and we hastened to quit the town, our game bags on our backs, our guns upon our shoulders. I know not what kind of game we chased; we went along, idling in the dew, running amid the tall grass which bent down beneath our feet with sharp and quick sounds; we wallowed in the country like young colts escaped from the stable. Our game bags were empty on our return, but our minds were full and our hearts also.

What a delicious district is Provence, biting and mild for those who are penetrated by its ardor and tenderness! I remember those white, damp and almost cool dawns, which filled my being and the sky above with the peace of supreme innocence; I remember the overwhelming sun of noon, the hot, heavy and fragrant atmosphere which weighed down upon the earth, those broad rays which poured from the heights like gold in fusion—virile and powerful hour, giving to the blood a precocious maturity and to the earth a marvellous fertility. We walked like brave children amid those dawns and scorching noons, young and frisky in the morning, but grave and more thoughtful in the evening; we talked in brotherly fashion, sharing our bread together and experiencing the same emotions.

The lands were yellow or red, desert and desolate, sown with slender trees; here and there were groves of foliage, of a dark green, staining the broad gray stretch of the plain; then, in the distance, all around the horizon, were low hills ranged in an immense circle, full of jagged spots, of a light blue or a pale violet, standing out with a delicate sharpness against the dark, deep blue of the sky. I can still see those penetrating landscapes of my youth. I well know that I belong to them, that what little of love and truth is in me comes to me from their tranquil delights.

At other times, towards evening, when the sun was sinking, we took the broad white highway which leads to the river. Poor river, meagre as a brook, here narrow, troubled and deep, there broad and flowing in a sheet of silver over a bed of stones. We chose one of the hollows, on the edge of a lofty bank which the waters had eaten away, and in it we bathed beneath the overhanging branches of the trees. The last rays of the sun glided between the leaves, sowing the sombre shade with luminous specks, and rested upon the bosom of the river in broad plates of gold. We perceived only water and verdure, little corners of the sky, the summit of a distant mountain, the vineyards in a neighboring field. And we lived thus in the silence and the coolness. Seated upon the bank, in the short grass, with legs hanging and bare feet splashing in the water, we enjoyed our youth and our friendship. What delicious dreams we indulged in upon those shores, the gravel of which was being gradually borne away every day by the waves! Our dreams vanish thus, borne away by the resistless current of life!

To-day these remembrances are harsh and implacable towards me. At certain hours, in my idleness, a remembrance of that age will suddenly come to me, sharp and dolorous, with the violence of a blow from a club. I feel a burning sensation running across my breast. It is my youth which is awakening in me, desolate and dying. I take my head in my hands, restraining my sobs; I plunge with a bitter delight into the history of those vanished days and take pleasure in enlarging the wound, the while repeating to myself that all this is no more and will never be again. Then, the recollection vanishes; the lightning has passed over me; I am overwhelmed with grief, recalling nothing.

Later still, at the age when the man awakens in the child, our life changed. I prefer the first hours to those hours of passion and budding virility; the recollections of our hunting excursions, of our vagabond existence, are more agreeable to me than the far off vision of young girls, whose visages remain imprinted on my heart. I see them, pale and indistinct, in their coldness, their virgin indifference; they passed by, knowing me not, and, to-day, when I dream of them again, I say to myself that they cannot dream of me. I know not how it is, but this thought makes them strangers to me; there is no exchange of recollections, and I regard them in the light of thoughts alone, in the light of visions which I have cherished and which have vanished.

Let me also recall the society which surrounded us: those professors, excellent men, who would have been better had they possessed more youth and more love; those comrades of ours, the wicked and the good, who were without pity and without soul like all children. I must be a strange creature, fit only to love and weep, for I was softened and suffered from the time I first walked. My college years were years of weeping. I had in me the pride of loving natures. I was not loved, for I was not understood and I refused to make myself known. To-day, I no longer have any hatred; I see clearly that I was born to tear myself with my own hands. I have pardoned my former comrades who ruffled me, wounded me in my pride and in my tenderness; they were the first to teach me the rude lessons of the world, and I almost thank them for their harshness. Among them were sorry, foolish and envious lads, who must now be perfect imbeciles and wicked men. I have forgotten even their names.

Oh! let me, let me recollect. My past life, at this hour of anguish, comes to me with a singular sensation of pity and regret, of pain and joy. I feel myself deeply agitated, when I compare all that is with all that is no more. All that is no more are Provence, the broad, open country flooded with sunlight, you, my tears and my laughter of other days; all that is no more are my hopes and dreams, my innocence and pride. Alas! all that is are Paris with its mud, my garret with its poverty; all that is are Laurence, infamy, my tenderness and love for that miserable and degraded woman.

Listen: it was, I believe, in the month of June. We were together on the brink of the river, in the grass, our faces turned towards the sky. I was talking to you. I have this instant recollected my words, and the remembrance of them burns me like a red hot iron. I had confided to you that my heart had need of purity and innocence, that I loved the snow because it was white, that I preferred the water of the springs to wine because it was limpid. I pointed to the sky; I told you that it was blue and immense like the clear, deep ocean, and that I loved the ocean and the sky. Then, I spoke to you of woman; I said I would have preferred that she were born, like the wild flowers, in the open air, amid the dew, that she were a water plant, that an eternal current washed her heart and her flesh. I swore to you that I would love only a pure girl, a spotless innocent, whiter than the snow, more limpid than the water of the spring, deeper and more immense in purity than the sky and the ocean. For a long while, I held forth enthusiastically to you thus, quivering with a holy wish, anxious for the companionship of innocence and immaculate whiteness, unable to pause in my dream which was soaring towards the light.

At last, I possess a companion, a spotless innocent! She is beside me and I love her. Oh! if you could see her! She has a sombre and unfeeling visage like a clouded sky; the waters were low and she has bathed in the mud. My spotless innocent is soiled to such an extent that formerly I would not have dared to touch her with my finger, for fear of dying therefrom. Yet I love her.

I am laughing; I feel a strange delight in jeering at myself. I dreamed of luxury, and I have no longer even a morsel of cloth with which to clothe myself; I dreamed of purity, and I love Laurence!

Amid my poverty, when my heart bled and I realized that I loved, my throat was choked, terror seized upon me. Then it was that my remembrances rose up. I have not been able to drive them away; they have remained with me, implacable, in a crowd, tumultuous, all entering simultaneously into my breast and burning it. I did not summon them; they came and I yielded to them. Every time I weep, my youth returns to console me, but its consolations redouble my tears, for I dream of that youth which is dead forever.

XVII

CLAUDE'S LOVE

I cannot stop, I cannot lie to myself. I had resolved to hide my misfortune from myself, to seem ignorant of my wound, hoping to forget. One sometimes kills death in its germ when one believes in life.

I suffer and weep. Without doubt, by searching within myself I will find a lamentable certainty, but I prefer to know everything to living thus, affecting a carelessness which costs me such great effort.

I wish to ascertain to what point of despair I have descended; I wish to open my heart and there read the truth; I wish to penetrate to the utmost depths of my being, to interrogate it and to demand from it an account of itself. At least, I ought to discover how it happens that I have fallen so low; I have the right to probe my wound, at the risk of torturing myself and ascertaining that I must die of it.

If, in this disagreeable task, I should make my wound greater than it is, if my love should increase by affirming itself, I will accept this augmented pain with joy, for the brutal truth is necessary to those who walk unshackled in life, obeying only their instincts.

I love Laurence, and I exact from my heart the explanation of this love. I did not fall in love with her at first sight, as men fall in love with women in romances. I have felt myself attracted little by little, melted, so to speak, gnawed and covered gradually by the horrible affliction. Now, I am altogether under its influence; there is not a single fibre of my flesh which does not belong to Laurence.

A month ago I was free; I kept Laurence beside me as one keeps an object which one cannot cast into the street. At present, she has bound me to her; I watch over her, I gaze at her when she is wrapped in slumber; I do not wish her to leave me.

All this was decreed by fate, and I think I can comprehend how love for this woman entered into me, took slow possession of my entire being. Amid suffering and abandonment, one cannot live with impunity beside a woman who suffers as one does, who is abandoned as one is. Tears have their sympathy, hunger is fraternal; those who are dying together, with empty stomachs, warmly grasp each other's hands.

ÉMILE ZOLA

I have remained five weeks in this sad and cold chamber, always in Laurence's company. I saw only her in the whole world; she was for me the universe, life, affection. From morning till night, I had before my eyes the face of this woman upon which I imagined I sometimes surprised a rapid flash of friendship. As for me, I was wretched and weak; I lived wrapped in my coverlet, an exile from society, not even possessing the power to go to seek my portion of the sunlight. I no longer had the smallest hope of anything; I had limited my existence to these four dark walls, to that corner of the sky which I saw between the chimney tops; I had fastened myself up in my dungeon, I had there imprisoned my thoughts, my wishes. I know not if you can thoroughly understand this: if you are some day without a shirt, you will realize that man can create a world, vast and full of living beings, from the bed upon which he is stretched.

I was in that condition when I met a woman as I went from the window to the door, enveloped in my coverlet. Laurence, seated in her chair, saw me walking about for hours together. Each time I trudged back and forth, I passed before her and found her eyes tranquilly following me. I felt her glance fasten itself upon me, and I was solaced in my weariness. I cannot tell what intense and strange consolation I derived from knowing myself regarded by a living creature, by a woman. It is from the period of these glances that my love must date. I perceived for the first time that I was not alone; I felt a profound satisfaction in discovering a human creature near me.

This creature was, without doubt, at first only a friend. I finally sat down beside her, talked, and wept without concealing my tears. Laurence, whom my sad situation and extreme poverty must have filled with pity, answered me, wiped away my tears. She also was weary of thus dying by inches; the silence and cold had at last begun to be tiresome to her. Her words seemed to me more refined, her gestures more caressing than usual; she had almost become a woman again.

At this point, brothers, I was suddenly invaded by love. My sphere of life was growing narrower each day. The earth was fleeing from me; Paris, France, yourselves, my thoughts and my acquaintances, all were no more. Laurence represented in my eyes God and mankind, humanity and the Divinity; the chamber in which she was had acquired a horizon out of all proportion. I felt myself beyond the world, almost in the embrace of death; I no longer thought that I might one day descend into the street, the noise of which mounted to my ears, and I had so little comprehension that I was alive that the thought had come to me to live without eating. It seemed to me that Laurence and I were in another part of the celestial system, lost, separated from the living, transported to some unknown corner beyond time and space. We could not have been more alone in the midst of the infinite.

One evening, as twilight came on, filling the chamber with a transparent gloom, I was walking slowly about, still going from the door to the window. In the growing obscurity, I saw Laurence's pale face, standing out from amid her dishevelled black hair; her sombre eyes had a vague brightness, and she looked at me thus, steadily, beautiful in her sufferings. I stopped in my weary walk and contemplated her. I knew not what had taken place within me; my flesh was shaken, my heart was open and I trembled like a leaf in every limb. All of a quiver, I ran to Laurence and clasped her in my arms. I loved her.

I loved Laurence with all the strength of my abandonment and poverty. I was suffering from hunger and cold, I was clad in a rag of wool, I felt myself forsaken by everybody, and yet I had a sweetheart to fold to my bosom, to love with the love of desperation! In the depths of infamy, I had found the sweetheart who was waiting for me. Now, in the gulf, far removed from the light, we were alone to embrace, to clasp each other, like children who are afraid and who reassure themselves by hiding their heads on each other's shoulders. What silence was around us, and what gloom! How sweet it is to love in solitude, amid those deserts of despair whither all sounds of life have ceased to penetrate! I plunged to the depths of this supreme felicity; I loved Laurence with the caressing delight with which the dying man must love the existence which is escaping from him.

I passed a week in a sort of dolorous ecstasy. I was tempted to stop up the window, that we might live in the midst of darkness for the balance of our lives; I wished to shut out the entire world and all it contained; I wished that the garret were very much smaller, so small, in fact, that no intruder could ever get into it to remind us that we were mortal like the rest of mankind and womankind. I did not think myself sufficiently miserable; I wanted more wretchedness, an excess of affliction of the most biting and terrible description; I desired the advent of some frightful misfortune that should strip me of all that want had left, that should tear from me every remaining comfort and leave Laurence and myself to live without having to thank this earth for anything whatever! I sighed for perfect independence and complete isolation. Then, my days would sweep by, each in its turn plunging me deeper into my love and my poverty. I was enraptured with cold and hunger, with the dirty mansarde, with the stains upon the walls and the furniture. I was enraptured with the blue silk dress, that lamentable assemblage of soiled tatters. My heart almost burst with pity when I saw Laurence standing before me, with this rag upon her back; I asked myself with the utmost anxiety by what kiss, by what superhuman kindness, I could clearly and unmistakably prove to her that I adored her in her poverty. As for me, I was happy in possessing only my coverlet: I would be colder, I would suffer more. I recall those first days like some strange, bewildering dream; I see the mansarde more in disorder, gloomier than ever, I breathe the thick and suffocating atmosphere which the window did not renew; I see Laurence and myself, like shadowy ghosts, walking about the miserable garret in our repulsive rags, chatting lovingly together, living in ourselves.

Yes, I love her, I love her desperately. I interrogate myself, and my palpitating heart narrates to me the horrible story, telling me how it came about. I have enlarged my wound; now that I have searched within myself, now that I know the reason and the depth of my love, I feel that I have more fever, that I have become mad and reckless.

A short time ago, I was shocked at the very thought of loving Laurence. My pride is dead, for I am shocked no longer. I have descended to Laurence's level; I understand her perfectly now, and do not wish her to be other than she is. I take a savage joy in saying to myself that I am now at the very bottom of the social scale, that I am satisfied there, and that there I will remain. I appreciate Laurence the more because of the gay and careless life she led in the past. There is, I know, despair, a sort of bitter irony, in my love; I have the intoxication of evil, the delirium of abandonment and hunger; I give myself up to the existence which has suddenly welcomed me, in order to insult the light on which my soul dotes and to which I cannot ascend.

Did I not at one time speak of redemption? I wished to reform Laurence, to lead her into better ways, to make her good and useful. What an insane idea! It was much easier for me to become unworthy. To-day, we love each other. Poverty betrothed us, agony married us. I love Laurence in all her ugliness and wretchedness, I love Laurence in her blue silk rag, in her rough degradation. I do not wish another sort of a Laurence, I do not wish a spotless innocent with a white soul and rosy countenance.

I do not know what are my companion's thoughts, I do not know whether my kisses delight or fatigue her. She is paler and graver than of old. With closed lips, staring eyes and expressionless face, she returns my caresses with a sort of repressed strength. Sometimes, she seems weary, as if she were discouraged at searching for something which she could not find; but soon she appears to resume her task and search anew, looking me in the face, her hands upon my shoulders. Besides, she has still the same weary appearance, the same dull soul; she sleeps constantly with her eyes open, and awakes with a start when I place my lips upon hers. When I told her of my love, she showed considerable astonishment, then, for two weeks, she lived a younger and more active life; a few days ago, she fell back into her eternal sleep.

But what difference does this make to me? I do not as yet feel that I need Laurence to love me. I am at that point of supreme selfishness which, in love, is satisfied with its own tenderness. I love and desire nothing more; I forget myself in the society of this woman and ask no other consolation.

XVIII

JACQUES' SUPPER

L ast evening, there was a grand fête at Jacques' apartment. Pâquerette came in the afternoon to tell us that our neighbors expected us to supper at eleven o'clock. Imprisoned as I was for lack of clothing, I did not refuse the invitation, being desirous of procuring some amusement for Laurence.

After Pâquerette's departure, we debated the important question of pantaloons. It was decided that Laurence should cut me out a pair of short breeches from a piece of green serge, which had long lain about upon the floor. She went to work, and, two hours afterwards, I was costumed like a lighterman in a shirt of doubtful whiteness, with a strip of damask around my waist to support my breeches.

Laurence then cleaned her blue silk dress, as much as possible, with a dampened rag. She brightened it up by stretching the stuff over one of her knees and rubbing it; she even pushed the repairs so far as to sew around the sleeves and corsage a little lace, which had once been white but was now yellow and rumpled.

Our entrance was triumphal. Jacques and Marie pretended to believe that a bit of pleasantry was intended; they applauded us, as actors are applauded who attain the effect they desire to produce. I was a trifle ashamed; I did not feel at ease until no one paid any further attention to my short breeches of green serge.

We found Pâquerette installed in an arm-chair. I know not how that little old woman ever managed to get into the apartment of Jacques, who is a cold young man and but little of a talker. She has the suppleness of a serpent and a honeyed and trembling voice which force the best closed doors. She appeared perfectly at home; she spread herself out carefully, passing her dry hands over her skirts, partially throwing back her head, opening and shutting her gray eyes lost among the wrinkles of her face. She seemed to taste in advance the delicacies placed beside her on a table.

Marie, who had arisen on our arrival, seated herself again in a corner of the sofa; the flushes on her cheeks shone more brightly than usual, and she laughed, displaying her white teeth. Jacques, standing before the mantelpiece, politely listened to what she had to say, always grave but affectionate, almost smiling.

They had brought forward chairs for us. The chamber was brilliantly lighted by two candelabra, each containing five candles, placed upon the table. This table, loaded with bottles and plates, had been pushed against the wall to make room, there to await its opportunity to occupy the middle of the apartment. The curtains of the bed were drawn; the floor, the hangings and the furniture seemed to have been brushed and washed with care. We were in the midst of luxury, in the midst of festivity.

I was about to participate, for the first time, in one of those suppers of which I had formerly dreamed in Provence. I was calm and self-possessed. Laurence smiled and I was happy in her joy. There is in the brightness of candles, in the sight of bottles red with wine, of plates full of cakes and cold meats, in the sensation produced by a close chamber, luminous and saturated with indefinable perfumes, a sort of physical comfort which puts thought to sleep. My companion, her lips parted, had, doubtless, again found well-known odors in that apartment. As for me, I felt the blood flow with increased warmth and rapidity in my veins; I experienced an inclination to laugh and drink, urged on by my now thoroughly awakened nature.

Besides, the chamber was quiet, the bursts of gayety softened, the entertainment decent and orderly. We drank a glass of Madeira, talking with the utmost calmness. This tranquillity made me impatient, I was tempted to cry out. The two young women had taken places beside Pâquerette, and the trio were conversing in low tones. I heard the broken voice of the old woman like a murmur, while Jacques was explaining to me the reason of the festival. He had just passed an examination successfully and was celebrating the event. He was more expansive and less the practical man than usual; he abandoned his customary gravity further, forgetting to talk of his future position, going even so far as to speak of his youth. Jacques, to tell the plain truth, was intoxicated with joy; he consented to play the fool, because he was a step higher up on the ladder leading to wisdom.

Finally we went to table. I had waited for this moment. I filled my glass and drank. I was exceedingly hungry, as was natural with a man who lived on crusts; but I disdained the cakes and the cold meats; I turned my attention to the wine, white or red. I did not drink from need of intoxication, I drank for the sake of drinking, because it seemed to me that I was there to empty my glass. I acquitted myself of that task most conscientiously, and I experienced a sensation of joy on feeling my limbs grow weaker little by little and my ideas become confused.

At the expiration of half an hour, the flames of the candles paled and spread out, the chamber grew red in every part, a dim and vacillating red. My reason, which had been wavering, was strengthened in a strange fashion; it had acquired a frightful lucidity. I was intoxicated; I must have had upon my countenance the stupid mask and idiotic smile of drunkards; but, within me, in the depths of my intelligence, I felt myself calm and sensible, I reasoned in full liberty. It was a terrible species of drunkenness; I suffered from the weakening of my body, which was greatly overcome, and from the vigor of my mind, which saw and judged.

Amid the clatter of glasses and forks, I looked at the women and Jacques, who were laughing and chatting among themselves. Their visages and their words came to me sharply and clearly, producing a sensation painful in its sharpness and penetration. My love was still in me, troubling and transforming my being; but the man of other days, the philosophical reasoner, had been again awakened. I took delight in my intoxication and in Laurence, at the same time thoroughly comprehending the nature of these two disgraces.

Jacques was seated at my left; I know not if he had succeeded in intoxicating himself; however, he feigned to be under the influence of liquor. Seated opposite to me were the three women, Marie on my right, then Pâquerette, then Laurence, who was on Jacques' left. My looks were fixed upon these women, who seemed to me to possess new visages and tones of voice.

I had not seen Marie since the day I had found her upon the sofa, white and languishing. Then, she looked like a young girl in the last stage of consumption. Now, her flaxen locks hanging loosely, her face flushed with excitement, her cheeks tinged with a pale violet, she agitated her bare arms with the fever of an ignorant child who is marching to her first delight. I was bewildered by the brightness of her youthful countenance.

I cannot describe the painful sensation produced in me by this creature, who had thrown off her agony to laugh and drink, to try to enjoy the delicious anguish of that life which she had unconsciously lived in her childish innocence. As I stared at her, quivering and with her hair thus dishevelled, her eyes flashing and her lips humid, it seemed to me, in the bewilderment of my intoxication, that I was gazing upon some expiring creature, who, on her death bed, suddenly hears the voice of her senses and her heart, and who, hesitating, not knowing what to do at that supreme moment, nevertheless does not wish to die before having satisfied her vague longings.

Laurence also had grown exceedingly animated. She was almost beautiful amid her unwonted excitement. Her visage had assumed a terrible expression of frankness and abandonment, which imparted to each of her features a look of the utmost insolence; her entire countenance had become lengthened; broad, square sections, crossed by deep lines, divided in a marked manner her cheeks and throat into firm and disdainful masses. She was pale, and several beads of perspiration stood on her forehead at the roots of her hair which was puffed straight up on her low, flat head. Reclining in her arm-chair, her face dead and distorted, her eyes black and glowing, she appeared to me like the frightful image of a woman who has weighed in her hand all the delights of the world and who now refuses them, finding them too light. At times, I fancied that she looked at me, shrugging her shoulders, that she smiled on me in pity, and that I heard her say to me, in a hoarse and horrid whisper: "So you love me, do you? What do you want of me? Physically I am no more than a corpse, and as for a heart, I never had one!"

Pâquerette looked thinner and more wrinkled than I had ever seen her before. Her face, like a dried apple, seemed to be more wasted than usual and had acquired a faint tinge of brick red. Her eyes were no longer anything but two brilliant points. She wagged her head in a mild and amiable way, chattering like a sharp-toned bird organ. She enjoyed, besides, perfect calmness, although she alone had eaten and drunk as much as all the rest of us together.

I stared at all three of them. The confusion of my brain, which exaggerated their dimensions, made them oscillate strangely before me. I said to myself that every species of dissipation was represented at this festival: youthful and careless dissipation, dissipation ripe in its frankness, dissipation which has grown old and lives amid its whitened locks on the remembrance of its follies of other days. For the first time, I saw these women together, side by side. They alone were a whole world in themselves. Pâquerette ruled, as became her old age; she presided; she called the two unfortunates who caressed her "my daughters." There was, however, intense cordiality between them; they talked to each other like sisters, without thinking of the difference in their ages. My bewildered glances confounded the three heads; I knew no longer above which forehead was the white hair.

Jacques and I were opposite to these women. We were young; we were celebrating a success of intelligence. I was on the point of quitting the apartment, brothers, and running to you. Then, I indulged in a burst of laughter, a very loud one, without doubt, for the women stared at me in astonishment. I said to myself that this was the kind of society amid which I was destined, for the future, to live. I closed my eyes and saw angels, clad in long blue robes, who were ascending in a pale light, full of sparks.

The supper had been exceedingly gay. We had sung and we had talked. It seemed to me that the chamber was filled with a thick smoke, which stopped up my throat and stung my eyes. Then, everything whirled about; I thought that I was going to sleep, when I heard a distant voice, which cried out, with the sound of a cracked bell:

"We must embrace each other! we must embrace each other!"

I half opened my eyes, and saw that the cracked bell was Pâquerette, who had just climbed upon her chair. She was shaking her arms and giggling.

"Jacques! Jacques!" cried she, "embrace Laurence! She is a good girl, and I give her to you to drive away your weariness! And you, Claude, poor sleepy child, embrace Marie, who loves you and offers you her lips! Come, let us embrace each other, let us embrace each other and amuse ourselves a trifle!"

And the little old woman sprang from her arm-chair to the floor.

Jacques leaned over and gave a kiss to Laurence, who immediately returned it. Then, I turned towards Marie, who, with outstretched arms and head thrown back, was waiting for me. I was about to kiss her on the forehead, when she threw her head still further back and offered me her mouth. The light of the candles fell upon her face. My eyes were fixed on her eyes, and I noticed in the depths of her glance a brightness of a pure blue tint which seemed to me to be her soul.

As I bent down, still contemplating Marie's soul, I felt the touch of cold lips on my neck. I turned instantly; Pâquerette was there, laughing, clapping her dry hands. She had embraced Jacques and had come to embrace me in my turn. I wiped my neck, with a shiver of disgust.

Seven o'clock struck; a wan brightness announced the advent of day. All was over; we had now nothing to do but to separate. As I was leaving the room, Jacques threw across my shoulder a coat and a pair of pantaloons which I did not even think of refusing. Pâquerette ascended the stairs in front of us, bearing a candle in her hand and holding aloft her thin arm that she might the better illuminate our way.

When we had reached our garret, I thought of the embraces we had exchanged. I looked at Laurence; I imagined that I saw her lips red from contact with Jacques' lips. I had still before me, in the gloom, the blue glimmer which had burned in the depths of Marie's eyes. I trembled, I knew not why, at the vague thoughts which came to me; then, I fell into a restless and feverish slumber. As I slept, I again felt on my neck the cold and painful sensation produced by Pâquerette's mouth; I dreamed that I passed my hand over my skin, but that I could not free myself from those frightful lips which were freezing me.

XIX

A Trip to the Country

Sunday, on opening the window, I saw that the spring had returned. The air had grown warmer, though it was yet somewhat chilly; I felt amid the last quivers of winter the first fervid glow of the sun. I breathed my fill of this wave of life rolling in the sky; I was delighted with the warm and somewhat biting perfumes which arose from the earth.

Each spring my heart is rejuvenated, my flesh becomes lighter. There is a purification of my entire being.

At the sight of the pale, clear sky, of a shining whiteness at dawn, my youth awakened. I looked at the tall wall; it was well-defined and neat; tufts of grass were growing between the stones. I glanced into the street: the stones and sidewalks had been washed; the houses, over which the rain storms had dashed, laughed in the sunlight. The young season had imparted its gayety to everything. I folded my arms tightly; then, turning around, I cried out to Laurence:

"Get up! get up! Spring is summoning you!"

Laurence arose, while I went out to borrow a dress and a hat from Marie, and twenty francs from Jacques. The dress was white, sown with lilac bouquets; the hat was trimmed with broad red ribbons.

I hurried Laurence, dressing her hair myself, so eager was I to get out into the sunlight. In the street, I walked rapidly, without lifting my head, waiting for the trees; I heard with a sort of thoughtful emotion the sound of voices and footsteps. In the Luxembourg Garden, opposite the great clusters of chestnut trees, my legs bent under me and I was compelled to sit down. I had not been out of doors for two months. I remained seated on the bench in the garden for a full quarter of an hour, in an ecstasy over the young verdure and the young sky. I had come out of darkness so thick that the bright spring bewildered and dazzled me.

Then, I said to Laurence that we would walk for a long, long while, straight ahead, until we could walk no longer. We would go thus into the warm but still moist air, into the perfumed grass, into the broad sunlight. Laurence, who had also been aroused by the revivifying influence of the balmy season, arose and drew me along, with hurried steps, like a child.

We took the Rue d'Enfer and the Orleans road. All the windows were open, displaying the furniture within the houses. Upon the thresholds of the street doors stood men in blouses, who engaged in friendly chat with each other while smoking. We heard bursts of hearty laughter coming out from the shops. Everything which surrounded me, streets, houses, trees and sky, seemed to me to have been carefully cleaned. The sky had an unusually enticing and new look, white with cleanliness and light.

At the fortifications, we encountered the first grass, short yet, but spread out like a vast carpet of light green and emitting a perfume intoxicating in its delicious freshness. We went down into the moat, making our way along beside the high gray walls, penetrating with curiosity into their secluded corners. On one side was the pale-hued stretch of wall, on the other the verdant slope. We advanced as if in a deserted and silent street which had no houses. In some of the corners the sun's rays had massed themselves, and had caused to shoot up tall thistles which were peopled by a whole nation of insects—beetles, butterflies and bees; these corners were full of buzzing sounds and grateful warmth. But, that morning, the slope threw its delightful shadow at our feet; we walked noiselessly upon a fine, thick turf, having before us a narrow band of sky, against which stood out in full light the meagre trees which rose above the wall.

The moats of the fortifications are little deserts, amid which I have very often forgotten myself and my troubles. The narrow horizon, the shade and the silence, which render more audible the hollow murmur of the great city and the bugles of the neighboring soldiers' barracks, make them peculiarly dear to boys, to little and grown up children. There, one is in an excavation at the gates of the city, feeling it pant and start, but no longer perceiving it. For half an hour, Laurence and I contented ourselves with this ravine which made us forget the houses and the beaten paths; we were a thousand leagues from Paris, far from every habitation, seeing only stones, grass and sky. Then, already suffocating, eager for the plain, we joyously ran up the slope. The broad country stretched out before us.

We found ourselves amid the airy and unconfined lands of Montrouge. These neglected and muddy fields are stricken with eternal desolation, poverty and lugubrious poesy. Here and there, the soil is

ÉMILE ZOLA

cleft frightfully, as with a horrible yawn, displaying, like open entrails, old and abandoned stone quarries, wan and deep. Not a tree is to be seen; huge windlasses alone stand out against the low, sad horizon. The lands have I know not what miserable aspect, and are covered with nameless wrecks. The roads twist, plunge into hollows and stretch away in a melancholy fashion. New huts in ruins and heaps of rubbish thrust themselves upon the eye at each turn of the paths. Everything has a raw look—the black lands, the white stones and the blue sky. The entire landscape, with its unhealthy aspect, its roughly cut up sections and its gaping wounds, has the indescribable sadness of countries which the hand of man has torn.

Laurence, who had become thoughtful in the moats of the fortifications, timidly clung to me as we were crossing the desolated plain. We walked on silently, sometimes turning to glance at Paris, which was grumbling in the distance. Then, we brought back our eyes to our feet, avoiding the gaps in the ground, contemplating with saddened souls this plain, the open wounds of which were brutally shown by the sun. Afar off were the churches, the Panthéons and the royal palaces; here were the ruins of an overturned soil, which had been searched and robbed to build these temples to men, to kings and to God. The city explained the plain; Paris had at its threshold the desolation which all grandeur causes. I know of nothing more mournful or more lamentable than those unconfined lands which surround great cities; they are not yet a part of the town and they are no longer the country; they have the dust, the mutilations of man, and have no longer the verdure or the tranquil majesty given them by God.

We were in haste to flee. Laurence had bruised her feet; she was afraid of this disorder, of this melancholy which reminded her of our chamber. As for me, I found in this wretched spot my love, my troubles and my bleeding life. We hurried away.

We descended a hill. The Bièvre river flowed along at the bottom of the valley, bluish and thick. Trees, here and there, bordered the stream; tall houses, sombre, narrow and pierced with immense windows, loomed up lugubriously. The valley was more discouraging than the plain; it was damp, oily and full of disagreeable smells. The tanneries there emitted sharp and suffocating odors; the waters of the Bièvre, that sort of common sewer open to the sky, exhaled a fetid and powerful stench which gave me a choking sensation. It was no longer the sad and gray desolation of Montrouge; it was the disgusting sight of a gutter, black with mud and refuse, bearing away with its waters horrible odors. A few poplar trees had grown vigorously in this reeking soil, and, above, against the clear sky, were pictured the long white lines of the Hôpital de Bicêtre, that frightful abode of madness and death, which worthily towers over the unhealthful and ignoble valley.

Despair seized upon me; I asked myself if I should not stop where I was and pass the day upon the borders of the sewer. I could not, it seemed, quit Paris, I could not escape from the gutter. Filth and infamy followed me even into the fields; the waters were corrupted, the trees had an unhealthy vigor, my eyes encountered only wounds and suffering. This must be the country which God now reserved for me. Each Sunday, I would come, with Laurence on my arm, to promenade upon the banks of the Bièvre, beside the tanneries, and to talk of love in that sink; I would come, at the noontide hour, to seat myself with my sweetheart on the oily ground, yielding to the awful influence of that dead creature and of the wretched valley. I paused in terror, ready to return to Paris on a run, and glanced at Laurence.

Laurence had her weighed down look, her look of want and premature old age. The smile she wore at her departure from the city had vanished. She seemed weary and dull; she looked around her, calmly, without disgust. I thought I saw her in our chamber; I realized that this slumbering soul needed more sunlight and nature of a gentler aspect to restore the innocence of a young girl's fifteenth year.

Then, I grasped her tightly by the arm; without permitting her to turn her head, I dragged her along, reascending the hill, always pushing straight ahead, following the roads, crossing the meadows, in quest of the young and virgin spring. For two hours we went along thus, in silence, rapidly. We passed two or three villages—Arcueil, Bourg-la-Reine, I believe; we hurried over more than twenty paths, between white walls and green hedges. Then, as we were about to leap across a narrow brook, in a valley full of foliage, Laurence uttered a childish shout, a burst of laughter, and escaped from my arm, running among the grass, all gayety, all innocence.

We were upon a large square of turf, planted with trees, with tall poplars, which arose like a jet of water, majestically, and balanced themselves languidly in the blue air. The turf was close and thick, dark in the shade and golden in the sunlight; one might have called it, when the wind agitated the poplars, a broad carpet of silk with changing reflections. All around extended cultivated lands, covered with shrubs

ÉMILE ZOLA

and plants: there was a sea of leaves at the horizon. A white house, low and long, which was in the shade, at the edge of a neighboring grove of trees, stood out gayly against all this green. Further away, higher up, on the edge of the sky, across the shadows, were seen the first roofs of Fontenay-aux-Roses.

The verdure was of recent growth, it had virgin freshness and innocence; the young leaves, pale and tender, in transparent masses, seemed like light and delicate lace placed upon the great blue veil of the sky. The tree trunks themselves, the rough old trunks, appeared as if newly painted; they had hidden their wounds beneath fresh moss. It was a universal song, a bright and caressing gayety. The stones and the lands, the sky and the waters, all appeared neat, vigorous, healthy and innocent. The recently awakened country, green and golden beneath the broad azure sky, laughed in the light, intoxicated with sap, youth and purity.

And amid this youth, this purity, ran Laurence in the full light, amid the flowing sap. She plunged into the grass, drank in the pure air; she had again found her fifteenth year upon the bosom of this country which had not been green fifteen days. The young verdure had refreshed her blood; the young sunlight had warmed her heart, given roses to her cheeks. All her being had awakened in this awakening of the earth; like the earth, she had resumed her innocence under the mild influence of the season.

Laurence, supple and strong, ran wildly about, carried away by the new life which was singing in her being. She lay down, she arose, with vivacity, bursting out laughing; she stooped to pick a flower, then fled between the trees, afterwards returning all in a rosy glow. Her entire face was animated; its features, unbent and rendered supple, had a healthful expression of genuine joy. Her laugh was frank, her voice sonorous and her gestures caressing. Seated, with my back against the trunk of a tree, I followed her with my eyes, white amid the grass, her hat fallen upon her shoulders; I was pleased with the pretty dress, so neat and light, which she wore chastely, and which gave her the air of a turbulent schoolgirl. She ran to me, threw me, stalk by stalk, the flowers she had gathered—marguerites and gold buttons, eglantines and lilies of the valley; then, she started off again, shining in the sunlight, pale and dim in the shade, like an insect buzzing in the light, without the ability to pause. She filled the grass and leaves with noise and motion; she peopled the secluded corner in which we were; the spring had assumed more brightness, more life, since this woman, who had as if by enchantment become a spotless child, had been laughing amid the verdure.

Fresh, blooming, all of a quiver, Laurence came to me and seated herself at my side. She was moist with dew; her bosom rose and fell quickly, full of young and fresh breath. From her came a delightful odor of grass and health. I had at last beside me a woman who lived abundantly, purely, looking straight at the light. I leaned over and kissed Laurence on the forehead.

She took the flowers, one by one, arranging them in a bouquet. The sun was ascending, the shadows were darker; around us reigned complete silence. Lying flat on my back, I gazed at the sky, I gazed at the leaves, I gazed at Laurence. The sky was of a dead blue; the leaves, already languishing, were sleeping in the sunshine; Laurence, with her head bent down, calm and smiling, was hurrying through her task with quick and supple movements. I could not take my eyes from that partially reclining woman, lost amid her skirts, her forehead in gilded shade, who seemed to me innocent and active, restored to her fifteenth year. I felt such peace, such deep joy, that I feared either to stir or speak; I lived in the thought that spring was in me, around me, and that Laurence was purity itself; I lost myself in this dream of the spotlessness of my sweetheart and the worthiness of my love. At length I loved a woman; that woman laughed, that woman existed; she possessed the healthful color and the frank gayety of youth. The miserable days of the past were no more, the future appeared to me with a calm and splendid brightness. My dreams of innocence and my love of light were about to be satisfied; from this hour, a life of ecstasy and tenderness would commence. I thought no more of the Bièvre, that black sewer upon the borders of which I had had the frightful temptation to sit down and embrace Laurence. I now wished to inhabit the white dwelling, down there, at the edge of the grove of trees, to live in it forever with my sweetheart, with my wife, amid the dew, amid the sunlight, amid the pure air.

Laurence had finished her bouquet and tied it with a sprig of grass. It was eleven o'clock, and we had not yet eaten anything. It was necessary for us to quit these trees, beneath which my soul had loved for the first time, and go in quest of an inn. I walked on ahead, across the country, through narrow paths bordered with fields of strawberry plants. Laurence followed me, holding up her skirts, forgetting herself at each hedge. Suddenly, at the turn of a road, we found what we were looking for.

The Coup du Milieu, the inn we entered, is situated in a corner of land between Fontenay and Sceaux, near the pond of Plessis-Piquet. From without, one sees only a grove, a patch of verdure, about twenty trees which have grown vigorously; on Sundays, a sound of knives and forks, of laughter and songs, floats from this immense nest. Within, when one has passed through the door surmounted by a broad sign placed across it, and when one has descended a gentle slope, one finds himself in an alley shaded by foliage, bordered by groves to the right and to the left; each of these groves is provided with a long table and two benches, fastened in the ground, reddened and blackened by the rain. At its further end, the alley widens; there is a glade, and a swing hangs between two trees.

The groves were silent and deserted. Men in blue blouses, peasants, were swinging; a huge dog was sitting gravely in the middle of the alley. Laurence and I sat down beneath an arbor, at a large table intended to accommodate twenty persons. It was almost dark under the leaves, the coolness was penetrating. In the distance, we saw, between the branches, the country shining in the sunbeams, sleeping beneath the first rays. The acacias of the grove had bloomed the previous day; the mild and sweet odor of their flower clusters filled the calm and caressing air.

A servant spread a napkin over the end of the table, in guise of a cloth; then we were served with what we had ordered, mutton chops, eggs, I cannot remember exactly what. The wine, contained in a small jug of bluish stone, rasped the throat; a trifle rough and sharp, it stimulated the appetite marvellously. Laurence literally devoured all that was placed before her; I did not recognize those beautiful and hungry white teeth, biting the bread, as my companion laughed aloud. Never had I eaten with such enjoyment. I felt myself light in soul and body; I surprised myself believing that I was yet a student of those old days, when we went to bathe in the little river and dine upon the grass of the bank. I loved the white linen on the black table, the shade of the foliage, the iron forks, the rude crockery ware; I looked at Laurence; I lived abundantly in the plenitude of my sensations, intensely enjoying everything which surrounded me.

At dessert, the chief cook came to receive our congratulations. He was a tall old man, a trifle bent, clad all in white. He wore a cotton cap, and had, pushed back upon his temples, two tufts of grayish and curled hair, among which a few curl papers had been forgotten. Laurence laughed for an hour at his excellent face, at once subtle and simple.

I cannot tell what we did to pass away the time until evening. The day was a day of sunshine, of bewilderment. I know not what paths we took, what shady spots we chose to rest in. There is, when I think of those hours of ecstasy, a dazzling splendor before my eyes. The remembrance of details is rebellious; my entire being has the sensation of a great felicity, of a grand light. It seems to me vaguely that Laurence and I forgot ourselves in the midst of a ravine, among the moss, seeing only a vast stretch of sky; we remained there, hand clasping hand, speaking but little, intoxicated with our new experience; our eyes, turned heavenward, were filled with brightness even to the point of blindness; we no longer saw anything save our hearts and our thoughts. But all this is, perhaps, a dream; my memory is treacherous—I am conscious only of having been blind, of having caught glimpses of thousands of stars amid the darkness.

In the evening, without knowing how, we again found ourselves at the Coup du Milieu. A crowd was there. Young women and young men filled the groves, making a great noise and confusion; white dresses, red and blue ribbons, stained the light green of the leaves; bursts of merry laughter gently rippled along amid the twilight. Candles had been lighted upon the tables, pricking with luminous points the growing obscurity. Some Tyrolese were singing in the middle of the alley.

We ate upon the end of a table, as in the morning, joining in the general laughter, making efforts to get out of ourselves. The noisy youth surrounding us frightened me a little; I thought I saw among my neighbors many Jacqueses and many Maries. Between the tree branches, I perceived a corner of the sky, pale and melancholy, as yet without stars; I experienced much difficulty in taking my eyes from the calm heavens to fix them upon the world of folly shouting around me. I remember now that Laurence appeared to be excited and troubled.

Then, silence was re-established; all the strangers had departed, and we were left alone. I had resolved to sleep at the Coup du Milieu that I might enjoy, on the morrow, the dew, the white brightness of the dawn. While the servants were making preparations to accommodate us, Laurence and I walked out into the garden, at the further end of which we seated ourselves upon a bench. The night was mild, starry and transparent; vague sounds arose from the earth; a horn, on a neighboring height, complained in a faint and caressing tone. The plain, with its great masses of black, motionless foliage, stretched out its mysterious limits; it seemed to sleep, quivering, agitated by a dream of love.

Our chamber was damp. It was on the ground floor, low, new and already degraded. Pieces of furniture were absent from their appointed places. On the ceiling lovers had traced their names by passing the flame of a candle over the plaster; the knotty and straggling letters spread out, broad and black. I took a knife, and, like a child, cut the date beneath a heart-shaped window which opened upon the country, without either grating or shutter.

The bed was excellent, if the chamber did not present a handsome appearance. In the morning, on awaking, while still half asleep, I saw, upon the wall facing me, a sight which I could not comprehend and which filled me with terror. The chamber was yet dark; in the midst of the darkness, on the wall, an enormous heart was bleeding. I imagined that I felt my breast empty, and despairingly began to search within me for my love. I felt my love biting at my vitals, and then I realized that the sun had risen and that its rays were pouring in copious floods through the heart-shaped window.

Laurence arose; we opened the door and the window. A current of coolness entered, bearing into the chamber all the odors of the delightful country. The acacias, planted almost at the threshold, exhaled a milder and sweeter perfume than on the preceding evening. The purity of dawn rested upon the sky and upon the earth.

Laurence drank a cup of milk, and, before returning to Paris, I expressed a desire to climb to the wood of Verrières, in order to carry back with me, in my heart, a breath of the pure air of the morning. Above, in the wood, we walked with lingering steps along the verdant paths. The forest was like a beautiful bride on the day after the wedding; it had delicious tears, a youthful languor, a damp coolness, lukewarm and penetrating perfumes. The sunlight at the horizon slipped along obliquely, between the trees, in broad sheets; there was I know not what mildness in those golden rays which rolled down to earth like supple and dazzling silken veils. And, amid the coolness, we heard the stir of the awakening wood, those thousands of little sounds which bear witness to the life of the springs and of the plants; above our heads floated the songs of birds, beneath our feet were the murmurs of insects; all around us were sudden cracklings, the gurgling noises of flowing waters, deep and mysterious sighs which seemed to issue from the knotty sides of the oak trees. We advanced slowly, feeling an intense and indescribable delight in lingering amid sunlight and shadow drinking in the fresh air, striving to seize the confused words which the hawthorns seemed to address to us as we passed by them. Oh! the gentle and smiling morning, all soaked with happy tears, all softened with joy and youth! The country had reached that adorable age when old Nature has for a few days the delicate grace of infancy.

I returned to Paris with Laurence on my arm, young and strong, intoxicated with light and spring, my heart full of dew and love. I loved worthily, as a true man should, and I believed that I was so loved in return.

XX

A Bitter Avowal

S pring has vanished; I have awakened from my dream.

I know not the limit of my pitiful childishness; I know not what miserable soul dwells within me. The reality penetrates me, shakes me; my flesh is either acutely tortured or wildly delighted by what is; I am like a body of exquisite sonorousness, which vibrates at the slightest sensation; I have a sharp and clear perception of the society which surrounds me. And my soul is pleased to refuse the truth; it escapes from my flesh, it disdains my senses, it lives elsewhere amid deception and hope. It is thus that I walk through life. I know and I see, I blind myself and I dream. While I advance beneath the rain, in the midst of the mud, while I am profoundly conscious of all the cold, of all the dampness, I can, by means of a strange faculty, make the sun shine, be warm, create for myself a mild and delicate sky, without ceasing to feel the gloomy sky which presses down upon my shoulders. I do not ignore anything, I do not forget anything. I live doubly. I carry into my dreams the same frankness which I carry into real sensations. I have thus two parallel existences, equally alive, equally intense—one which passes here below, in my poverty, another which passes above, in the immense and deep purity of the blue sky.

Yes, such is, without doubt, the explanation of my being. I comprehend my flesh, I comprehend my heart; I am conscious of my innocence and of my infamy, of my love for illusion and of my love for truth. I am a delicate machine made up of sensations—sensations of the soul and sensations of the body. I receive and give back, quiveringly, the slightest ray, the slightest odor, the slightest tenderness. I live on too lofty a plane, crying out my sufferings, stammering forth my ecstasies, in heaven and amid the mud, more crushed after each new bound, more radiant after each new fall.

The other day, amid the cool air, beneath the tall trees of Fontenay, my flesh was softened, my heart had the mastery. I loved and I believed myself loved in my turn. The truth escaped from me; I saw Laurence clothed in white, young and pure; her kiss appeared to me to have so much sweetness that it seemed to come from her soul. Now, Laurence is here, seated upon the edge of the bed; to see her, pale and sorrowful, in her soiled dress, makes my flesh quiver, my heart leap with indignation. The spring time has flown; Laurence has grown old, she does not love me. Oh! what a miserable child I am! I deserve to weep, for I cause my own tears.

What do I care for Laurence's ugliness, her infamy and her weariness! Let her be uglier, more infamous and more weary, but let her love me! I wish her to love me.

I regret neither the graces of her fifteenth year nor her youthful smile of the other day, when she ran about beneath the trees and was the good fairy of my youth. No, I regret neither her beauty nor her freshness; I regret the dream which led me to believe that her heart was in her caresses.

She is here, deplorable, crushed. I have, indeed, the right to exact that she shall love me, that she shall give herself to me. I accept her entire being, I want her as she is, asleep and weary, but I want her, I want her, with all my will, with all my strength.

I remember that I dreamed of reforming Laurence, that I wished her to possess more reason, more reserve. What do I care for reserve, what do I care for reason? I have no business with them now. I demand love, mad and lasting love. I am eager to have my love returned, I do not wish longer to love all alone. Nothing wearies the heart like caresses which are not returned. I gave this woman my youth, my hopes; I shut myself up with her in suffering and abjection; I forgot everything in the depths of our gloom, even the crowd and its opinions. I can, it seems to me, demand in exchange from this woman that she shall unite herself with me, that she shall join her destiny to mine amid the desert of poverty and abandonment in which we live.

Spring is dead, I tell you. I dreamed that the young foliage was growing green in the sunlight, that Laurence laughed madly amid the tall grass. I find myself in the damp darkness of my chamber, opposite Laurence who is sleeping; I have not quitted the wretched den, I have not seen either the eyes or the lips of this girl open. Everything is deception. In this crumbling of the true and the false, in this confused noise which life causes within me, I feel but a single need, a sharp and cruel need: to love, to be loved, no matter where, no matter how, that I may plunge headlong into an abyss of devotion.

Oh! brothers, later, if ever I emerge from the black night which holds me captive, and the caprice should seize upon me to relate to the crowd the story of my far off loves, I will, without doubt, imitate those weepers, those dreamers, who deck with golden rays the demons of their twentieth year and put wings upon their shoulders. We call the poets of youth those liars who have suffered, who have shed all their tears, and who, to-day, in their recollections, have no longer anything but smiles and regrets. I assure you that I have seen their blood, that I have seen their bare flesh, torn and full of pain. They have lived in suffering, they have grown up in despair. Their sweethearts were vile creatures, their love affairs had all the horrors of the love affairs of a great city. They have been deceived, wounded, dragged in the mud; never did they encounter a heart, and each one of them has had his Laurence, who has made of his youth a desolate solitude. Then, the wound healed, age came on, remembrance imparted its caressing charm to all the infamy of the past, and they wept over their morbid love affairs. Thus they have created a false world of sinful young women, of girls adorable in their carelessness and their triviality. You know them all—the Mimi Pinsons and the Musettes—you dreamed about them when you were sixteen, and, perhaps, you have even sought for them. Their admirers were prodigal; they accorded them beauty and freshness, tenderness and frankness; they have made them shining types of unselfish love, of eternal youth; they have thrust them upon our hearts, they have taken delight in deceiving themselves. They lie! they lie! they lie!

I will imitate them. Like them, without doubt, I shall deceive myself, I shall believe in good faith the falsehoods which my recollections will relate to me; like them, perhaps, I shall have cowardice and timidity which will induce me not to speak loudly and frankly, telling what were my love affairs and how utterly miserable they were. Laurence will become Musette or Mimi; she will have youth, she will have beauty; she will no longer be the mute, wretched woman who is now in my company—she will be a giddy young girl, loving thoughtlessly, but thoroughly alive, rendered more youthful and more adorable by her caprices. My den will be transformed into a gay mansarde, blooming, white with sunlight; the blue silk dress will be changed into a neat and graceful calico; my poverty will be full of smiles, my tenderness will sparkle like a diamond. And I will sing in my turn the song of my twentieth year, taking up the refrain where the others have left it, continuing the sweet and lying words, deceiving myself, deceiving those who shall come after me.

Brothers, in these letters written for you alone, which I prepare day by day, quivering yet from the terrible shocks I have received, I can be rough, sharp, revealing everything, emphasizing my confessions. I give myself up wholly, I spread my entire life out before you, I exhibit to you my flesh and my blood: I wish to take my heart from my breast, to show it to you, bleeding, sick, frank in its baseness and in its purity. I feel myself better and worthier in confessing myself to you; I have an immense pride amid my abasement; the deeper I descend, the more disdain, the more superb indifference, I acquire. What a delicious thing is frankness! Say to yourselves that, out of ten young men, eight have the same life, the same youth, as I: some two or three in a hundred, perhaps, become frightened and weep as I weep; the others, several thousands, accept their lot and live in peace, infamous and smiling. All lie. As for me, I wound myself, I admit to you with sobs what are my love affairs, and tell you with what a terrible weight they stifle me.

Later, I will lie.

Nothing exists now, except the love of Laurence, which I have not and which I exact. There is no more light, there is no longer a world, there is no longer a crowd; in the gloom, a man and a woman are brought face to face forever. The man, setting aside all his lofty aspirations, all his appreciation of beauty, wishes to be loved by the woman, because he is afraid of being alone, because he is cold and hungry, because he loves himself. At the final day, when humanity is expiring, and when but a single couple remain upon the earth, the struggle will be terrible, the despair immense, if the last adorer cannot awaken the last sweetheart from the dull sleep of the heart and the flesh.

XXI

A Horrible Proposition

Marie changed her chamber yesterday; she now lodges upon the same landing as I, in an apartment separated from mine by a simple partition. The poor child is dying; she gives vent to a light and hollow cough, with a sort of rattling in her throat after each attack of coughing. Jacques, whose studious quietude was disturbed by this cough, decided that the invalid would be more at her ease alone in a separate chamber. He has engaged Pâquerette to watch over and take care of her.

Last night, I heard for long hours Marie's cough and the rattling in her throat. Laurence slept on tranquilly. The sound of each half stifled fit which passed through the partition filled me with indescribable sadness.

This morning, on arising, I went to see the dying girl. She was in bed, white, resigned, still smiling. Her head, raised upon two pillows, had a sort of gentle languor; her thin and almost transparent arms were stretched out on the sheet beside her poor body, the sharp and lamentable outlines of which could be seen beneath the covers.

The chamber was dark and cold. It resembles mine, but is better furnished, less dirty. A large window opens upon the high wall, which looms up gloomily a few mètres from the front of the house.

Marie was alone, motionless, her eyes wide open, staring at the ceiling with that pensive and heart-rending air of invalids who already see beyond life. Pâquerette had just gone down-stairs to get her breakfast. On a small table, placed near an arm-chair, were an army of bottles, a single glass and the remains of food. The thought came to me that Pâquerette took more care of herself than of the dying girl.

I kissed Marie's forehead; I seated myself upon the edge of the bed, taking and holding one of her hands. She turned her head slowly and smiled upon me, telling me that she was not in pain, that she was resting herself. Her voice, a trifle hoarse, was reduced to a feeble and caressing murmur. Her forehead inclined, she looked at me with her feverish and enlarged eyes; astonishment and tenderness were mingled in her full glances. My heart was wrung with pity at the sight of this poor creature. I felt that I was on the point of bursting into tears.

Pâquerette returned, loaded with new bottles and fresh food. She opened the window, complaining of the bad air; she established herself comfortably in the arm-chair, before the table; then, she began to eat noisily, talking as she chewed, questioning Marie about her adorers, about her past life. She seemed to ignore that the poor girl was sick; she treated her like a lazy creature who loves to lie in bed and be pitied. I looked with disgust at this woman, wrapped up in herself, licking her greasy fingers, chuckling, bantering the dying girl with her mouth full, and casting at me sullen and cynical glances, those desperate glances which certain old women yet have in their reddened eyes.

Pâquerette, ceasing to eat, partially turned her arm-chair; then, crossing her hands upon her skirts, she looked at us, at Marie and myself, first at one and afterwards at the other, laughing a wicked laugh.

"Ah! my dear," said she to the sick girl, pointing at me her bony finger, "isn't he a handsome young fellow! His heart is widowed and has need of new love affairs!"

Marie smiled sadly, closing her eyes, withdrawing her hand which mine had kept.

"You are deceived," I answered Pâquerette, after a moment's silence; "my heart is not widowed. I love Laurence."

Marie lifted her eyelids, and restored to me her fingers, which I found more agitated, hotter, than before.

"Laurence! Laurence!" sneered the old woman; "she is making a fool of you! You are like all the rest of the men. They love those who betray and abandon them. Look for another sweetheart, my poor Monsieur, look for another sweetheart!"

I did not hear distinctly, according ordinarily no attention whatever to the chatter of this old woman. And yet, though I know not why, I felt a vague uneasiness. An unknown warmth filled my being with a painful quiver.

"Listen, my children," added Pâquerette, taking her ease: "I am a kind hearted woman, and it displeases me to see you made game of. You are very nice, both of you, gentle as lambs, good as bread. It has been my dream to see you married, and I well know that two better little creatures were never brought together. So, Monsieur, accept Madame. Every day, I meet Laurence and Jacques caressing each other on the stairway!"

I glanced at Marie. She was calm; the beating of her pulse had not increased. She seemed to be dreaming with her eyes fixed on me, and, perhaps, she saw me in her dream. The kisses which Jacques might have given to Laurence did not disturb the tranquil friendship which she felt for him.

As for me, I felt the insupportable warmth mount to my breast and stifle me. I knew not what was the sudden numbness which gave me a dull, deep pain, penetrating even to my soul. I thought neither of Laurence nor Jacques; I listened to Pâquerette and the suffocation augmented, stopping up my throat.

Pâquerette slowly rubbed her withered hands; her gray eyes, sunken beneath her flabby eyelids, shone strangely in her yellow visage. She resumed, in a voice more cracked than ever:

"You stare at each other like a couple of stupid innocents! Have you not understood, Claude? Jacques has taken Laurence from you; take Marie. Ah! the little one smiles: she asks nothing better. In the way I suggest, no one will be left disconsolate, no one will have any reproaches to make. That's the fashion in which everything should be arranged in this life!"

Marie impatiently lifted her hand, making her a sign to stop. The old woman's sharp voice imparted a quiver to her emaciated flesh. Then, her countenance assumed an expression of melancholy peace, an air of calm ecstasy; she gazed at me thoughtfully, and said to me, in a penetrating tone, a tone which I had never known her voice to possess:

"Will you, Claude? I will love you so much!"

And she sat upright.

A fit of coughing threw her back upon the bed, her body horribly shaken, all panting with pain. With arms open and twisted, with head thrown backward, she was suffocating. Her partially uncovered breast, that poor breast which suffering had made so infantile, so pure, rose and fell frightfully as if torn by a furious tempest. Then, the terrible cough passed away, and the girl stretched herself out, pale, her cheeks violet, as if overwhelmed with fatigue and insensibility.

I had remained seated upon the edge of the bed, shaken myself by the torture of the dying girl. I had not dared to stir, nailed to my place by pity and fright. What I had before me was so profoundly horrible and so infinitely touching, so lamentable and so repulsive, that I know not how to explain the holy fear which held me where I was, grieved, full of disgust and compassion. I was tempted to beat Pâquerette, to drive her away; I felt inclined to embrace Marie as a brother would embrace his sister, to give her my blood to restore life and freshness to her expiring flesh.

So I had reached this point: a miserable old woman, whose career had been one long dissipation, offered me the opportunity to exchange my heart for another heart, to give up my sweetheart to one of my friends and thus secure his of him; she showed me all the advantages of this bargain, she laughed at the excellent joke. And the sweetheart whom she wished to give me already belonged to death. Marie was dying, and Marie extended her arms to me. Poor innocent! her strange purity hid from her all the horror of her kiss. She offered her lips like a child, not understanding that I would rather have died than touch her mouth, I, who loved Laurence so much! Her pale flesh, burned by fever, had been purified by suffering; but she was already dead, so to speak, sanctified, and so pure that I would have deemed it sacrilegious to reawaken in her a final quiver of earthly delight.

Pâquerette curiously watched Marie's crisis. That woman does not believe in the sufferings of others.

"Something she ate choked her," she said, forgetting that the sick girl had swallowed no solid food for two weeks.

At these words, a blind rage took possession of me. I felt like slapping that yellow, sneering face, and, as the wretched creature opened her lips again:

"Be quiet, will you!" I cried out to her, in a ringing and indignant voice.

The old woman drew back her arm-chair in terror. She stared at me, full of fear and indecision; then, seeing that I was in earnest, she made a gesture such as a drunken man might make and stammered, in a drawling tone:

"Then, if joking is prohibited, why don't you say so in plain words? As for me, I always have a joke upon my lips, and so much the worse for those who weep say I! You don't want Marie; very well, let us say no more about it."

And she pushed the arm-chair before the table; then, she poured out a glass of wine, which she sipped slowly.

I bent over Marie, whom suffering had put to sleep. There was a low rattle in her throat. I kissed her on the forehead like a brother.

As I was about going away, Pâquerette turned towards me.

"Monsieur Claude," she cried, "you are not amiable, but, nevertheless, I will give you a piece of good advice. If you love Laurence, keep a sharp eye upon her!"

XXII

The Shadows on the Wall

I am jealous—jealous of Laurence!

That Pâquerette has filled me with the most frightful torment. I have descended, one by one, all the rounds of the ladder of despair; now, my infamy and my sufferings are complete.

I know the name of that unknown warmth which filled my breast and stifled me. That warmth was jealousy, a burning wave of anguish and terror. This wave has rolled upward, it has invaded my entire being. Now, there is no portion of me which is not in pain and jealous, which does not complain of the horrible pressure beneath which all my flesh cries out.

I know not in what manner others are jealous. As for me, I am jealous with all my body, with all my heart. When doubt has once entered into me, it watches, it works pitilessly; it wounds me every second, searches me, constantly making further encroachments. The pain is physical; my stomach is convulsed, my limbs grow heavy beneath me, my head feels hollow, weakness and fever seize upon me. And, above these afflictions of the nerves and muscles, I feel the anguish of my heart, deep and terrifying, which weighs me down, burns me incessantly. A single idea turns upon itself in the immense emptiness of my thoughts: I am no longer loved, I am deceived; my brain beats like a bell with this one sound, all my vitals have the same quiver, twisted and torn. Nothing could be more painful than these hours of jealousy which strike me doubly, in my body and in my affection. The suffering of the flesh and the suffering of the heart are united in a sensation of overwhelming weight, which is inexorable, crushing me constantly. And I hold my breath, abandoning myself, descending deeper and deeper into my suspicions, aggravating my wound, withdrawing myself from life, living only in the thought which is ruthlessly gnawing me.

If I suffered less, I would like to know of what my suffering is composed. I would take a bitter pleasure in interrogating my body, in questioning my tenderness. I am curious to see the uttermost depths of my despair. Without doubt, a thousand wretched things are there—love, selfishness, self-love, cowardice and evil passions, to say nothing of the rebellion of the senses, of the vanities of the intelligence. This woman who is going away from me, weary of my caresses, and who prefers another to me, wounds me in every portion of my being; she disdains me, she declares by her acts that she has found a love sweeter, purer, than mine. Besides, there is, above all, a feeling of immense solitude. I feel myself forsaken, I quiver with fright; I cannot live without this creature, whom I have taken pleasure in regarding as an eternal companion; I am cold, I tremble; I would rather die than remain deserted.

I exact that Laurence shall be mine. I have only her in the whole world, and I cling to her as a miser clings to his beloved gold. My heart bleeds when I think that, perhaps, Pâquerette is right, and that to-morrow I shall be shorn of love. I do not wish to remain all alone in my poverty, in the depths of my abjection. I am afraid.

And, nevertheless, I cannot close my eyes to the terrible reality, I cannot live in ignorance. Certain young men, when they feel that a woman is necessary to them, accept her such as she is; they do not care to risk their peace of mind by probing into her past life. So far as I am concerned, I realize that I have not sufficient strength to ignore anything. I doubt. My unfortunate mind urges me to disabuse or convince myself; I must know everything about Laurence, that I may die if she has resolved to abandon me.

In the evening, I pretend to go out for a walk, and slip furtively into Marie's apartment. Pâquerette is dozing; the dying girl smiles feebly upon me, without turning her head. I go to the window and there establish myself. From the window I keep a close watch, leaning out to see into the courtyard and into Jacques' chamber. Sometimes, I partly open the door and listen to the sounds on the stairway. These are cruel hours. My excited mind toils laboriously, my limbs tremble with anxiety and prolonged attention. When voices ascend from Jacques' chamber, emotion stops up my throat. If I hear Laurence leave our mansarde and she does not appear upon the threshold below, a burning sensation shoots through my breast: I have counted the steps, and I say to myself that she has stopped on the fourth floor. Then, I lean over into the courtyard at the risk of falling; I long to climb in through that window which opens five mètres below me. I imagine I hear the sound of kisses, I think I catch my name uttered amid mocking laughter. Then, when Laurence at last shows herself upon the threshold, in the courtyard, the burning sensation shoots through me again. I remain leaning out of the window, panting, broken. She surprises me, for I did not expect to see her. I commence to doubt: I no longer know if I correctly counted the steps she had to descend.

For a long while, I have played this cruel game with myself. I placed myself in ambush, and, the blood mounting to my eyes, I can no longer recall what I saw. Conviction flees from me; suspicions are born and die, more devouring each day. I have an infernal aptitude for spying out and arguing concerning the causes of my suffering; my mind greedily seizes upon the slightest facts; it masses them together, links them in a continuous chain, draws marvellous conclusions from them. I execute this little task with an astonishing lucidity; I compare, I discuss, I accept, I reject, like a veritable examining magistrate. But, as soon as I think I have possession of a certainty, my heart bursts out, my flesh quivers, and I am no more than a child who weeps on feeling the reality escape from him.

I would like to penetrate into the lives of my companions, to examine the mysteries; I am curious to analyze all I am ignorant of, I am strangely delighted by those delicate operations of the intelligence searching for an unknown solution. There is an exquisite enjoyment in weighing each word, each breath; one has but a few vague grounds for suspicion, and one arrives, by a slow, sure and mathematical march, at the knowledge of the entire truth. I can employ my sagacity in the service of my brethren. When I am concerned, however, I am agitated by such deep emotion that I am unable either to see or hear.

Last evening, I remained for two hours in Marie's chamber. The night was dark and damp. Opposite, upon the bare wall, Jacques' window threw a great square patch of yellow light. Shadows came and went in this square patch; they had a fantastic look and extraordinary dimensions.

I had heard Laurence close our door, and she had not gone down into the courtyard. I recognized Jacques' shadow on the wall, long and straight, tossing about with sharply defined and precise movements. There was another shadow, a shorter one, slower and more undecided in its motions; I thought that I also recognized this shadow, which seemed to me to have an unruly head increased in size by a woman's chignon.

At times, the square patch of yellow light stretched out, pale and wan, empty and calm. I leaned out of the window, breathlessly; I stared with painful attention, suffering from the emptiness and calmness of the light, wishing with anguish that a black mass would appear, betraying to me its secret. Then, suddenly, the square was peopled: a shadow passed over it, two shadows mingled together, out of all proportion and so strangely confused that I could neither seize the forms nor explain the movements. My mind sought with despair for the meaning of these dark stains which lengthened, broadened, sometimes permitting me to catch a partial glimpse of a head or an arm. The head and the arm instantly lost shape, melted into one perplexing spot of blackness. I no longer saw anything but a sort of oscillating wave of ink, spreading in every direction, smearing the wall. I strove to comprehend, and thought I distinguished monstrous silhouettes of animals, strange profiles. I lost myself in this distressing vision, this fearful nightmare; I followed with terror those masses which danced without noise; I trembled at the thought of what I was about to discover; I wept with rage on realizing that all this had no meaning whatever, and that I would learn nothing. Suddenly, the wave of ink, in a final leap, in a last contortion, flowed along the wall, along the darkness. The square patch of yellow light was again deserted and dull. The shadows had passed away, without revealing anything to me. I leaned forward, overflowing with despair, awaiting the terrible spectacle, saying to myself that my life depended upon those black stains which were capering about on the yellowed walls.

A sort of madness finally took possession of me in the presence of this ironical drama which was being played opposite to me. These strange personages, these rapid and incomprehensible scenes, mocked me; I wished to put an end to this lugubrious farce. I felt myself broken by emotion, devoured by doubt.

I quietly left Marie's chamber; I removed my shoes and placed them upon the landing; then, oppressed, anxious, I began to descend the stairway, pausing upon every step, hearing the very silence, frightened by the slightest sounds that mounted to me. Arrived in front of Jacques' door, after five long minutes of fear and hesitation, I bent down slowly, painfully, and heard the bones of my neck crack. I applied my right eye to the keyhole, but saw only darkness. Then, I glued my ear against the wood of the door: the silence seemed filled with buzzing sounds, but there was in my head a great murmur which prevented me from hearing distinctly. Flames passed before my eyes, a hollow and increasing rumbling filled the corridor. The wood of the door burned my ear, it appeared to me to be vibrating in every part. Behind that door I thought I caught at times half stifled sighs; then, death seemed to me to have passed through that chamber and left there intense and terrible silence. And I knew no more. I could tear nothing definite from the frightful stillness, from the oppressive gloom. I do not know how long I remained bent down against the door; I remember only that the icy coldness of the floor froze my feet and that a tremendous quaking shook my body, which was covered with a cold perspiration. Anguish and terror held me nailed to the spot, shrinking within myself, not daring to move, twisted by jealousy, quivering as if I had just committed a crime.

At last, I reascended the stairway, staggering, bruising myself against the walls. I again opened Marie's window, still having need of suffering, unable to withdraw myself from the biting delight of my torments. The wall opposite was a sheet of blackness; the curtain had fallen upon the drama, and night reigned. As I went out of the room, I gazed at Marie who was slumbering peacefully, with clasped hands. I believe that I knelt before the bed, addressing to I know not what divinity a prayer, the words of which came spontaneously to my lips.

I went to bed, shivering, and closed my eyes. I saw, through my eyelids, the glimmer of the candle, placed upon a little table opposite me, and I thus had a broad pink horizon which I peopled with lamentable figures. I possess the sad power of dreaming, the faculty of creating from fragments of every kind personages who almost breathe the breath of actual life; I see them, I touch them; they play like living actors the scenes which are passing through my mind. I suffer and I enjoy with greater intensity as my ideas materialize themselves and as I perceive them, my eyes closed, with all my senses, with all my flesh.

Amid the pink glimmer, I saw Laurence and Jacques. I saw the chamber which had appeared to me dark, silent, and now it was full of laughter, of brilliancy. My companion and my friend, in a flood of sparkling light, were chatting lovingly together; they sat there before my eyes, playing their rôles in the miserable drama which my dismayed mind dreamed. It was no longer a simple thought, an idea arising from heart jealousy, but a series of horrible, living pictures of frightful distinctness. I was shocked and cried out; I felt that the drama was being enacted within me, that I could veil these images, but I took a morbid delight in bringing them into bold relief, in giving their outlines greater clearness, in bestowing upon them the hues of actual life; I plunged at will into the horrible spectacle I had called up, that I might suffer further torture. My doubts were transformed into flesh and blood; I knew and I saw at last; I had found in my imagination the full certainty for which I had vainly searched at Marie's window and Jacques' door.

Laurence entered and shut the door roughly. She brought in with her from without an indescribable odor of tobacco and liquor. I did not open my eyes, listening to the sound of her footsteps and the rustling of her garments while she was disrobing. I looked at the pink glimmer, and, beyond it, it seemed to me that I saw this woman, when she passed before me, laugh in scornful pity and mock me with a gesture, believing that I was asleep.

She sat down in a chair, uttering a slight sigh, and leisurely concluded her preparations for the night. Then, all the pain I had experienced during that terrible evening returned and mounted to my throat. An utterly boundless rage took entire possession of me at the sight of this cold and treacherous creature calmly taking her ease, and seeming to have wholly forgotten me. I sat up in bed, clenching my fists.

"Where have you been?" I asked Laurence, in a hollow voice, trembling with anger.

She slowly opened her eyes, which were already half-closed, and stared at me for an instant, astonished, without replying. Then, with a shrug of her shoulders, she answered:

"I have been to the fruit-woman's up the street. She invited me yesterday to visit her, this evening, and drink coffee with her."

I saw her face from forehead to chin: her weary eyelids hung down, so heavy with sleep were they; her features wore an expression of satiety and satisfaction. I felt the blood blind me to see her so contented, caring so little for having forsaken me. Her neck, broad and puffed up, was extended towards me, soliciting me to commit a crime; it was thick and short, impudent and shameless; it shone insolently, mocking and defying me. Everything which surrounded me had disappeared; I no longer saw anything but that neck.

"You lie!" I cried.

And I seized the neck with my bent fingers, red flashes passing before my eyes. I shook Laurence violently, grasping her with all my strength. She did not offer the slightest resistance, but swayed to and fro beneath my hands, without a complaint, flabby and brutalized. I know not what pleasure I experienced on feeling her warm and supple body bend, yield to the force of my mad rage. Then, an icy shiver penetrated me and I was filled with fear: I thought I saw blood trickle along my fingers; I threw myself back upon the pillow, sobbing, intoxicated with grief.

Laurence put her hand to her neck. She took three long breaths; then, she sat down again, turning her back to me, without a word, without a tear.

I had shaken her hair loose. Upon the nape of her neck I perceived a bluish trace, made darker by the shadow of her locks which half concealed her shoulders. My tears blinded me, my heart was full of strong and tender compassion. I wept over myself who had just ill treated a woman, I wept over Laurence whose bones I had heard cry out beneath my fingers. My entire being was a prey to keen remorse; my tortured soul despairingly sought to repair what could never be forgotten. I recoiled, in disgust and fright, from the wild beast which I had felt awaken and die within me; I suffered from terror, shame and pity.

I approached Laurence; I clasped my arms around her, whispering in her ear, in a doleful and caressing tone. I know not what I said to her. My heart was full and I emptied it. My words were a long prayer, ardent and humble, meek and violent, overflowing with pride and baseness. I spoke of the past, of the present, of the future; I told the story of my heart, without the least reserve; I probed the utmost depths of my being, in order that I might hide nothing. I had need of pardon, I had also need of pardoning my companion. I accused Laurence, I demanded loyalty and frankness of her. I told her how much she had made me weep. I did not address reproaches to her the better to excuse myself; my lips opened in spite of me, all the present filled me, my daily thoughts united in a single tender and resigned complaint, free from even the least trace of anger, the least trace of animosity. My reproaches and confessions were mingled with sudden outpourings of love and tenderness; I spoke the puerile and indescribable language of excitement, soaring to the very sky, dragging myself along the ground; I made use of the adorable and ridiculous poesy of children and lovers; I was mad, passionate, intoxicated. And I went on thus, as in a dream, questioning, answering, speaking in a deep and regular voice, pressing Laurence against my bosom. For a whole hour I heard the words which, of themselves, flowed from my mouth, gentle, touching; I solaced myself by listening to this penetrating music; it seemed to me that my poor, wounded heart was rocking itself and putting itself to sleep.

Laurence, impassible, her eyes open, stared at the wall. My voice did not appear to reach her. She sat there as mute, as dead, as if she had been in the midst of thick darkness, in the midst of profound silence.

Her hard forehead, her cold and tightly closed lips, announced her firm resolution not to listen, not to reply.

Then, I felt a keen desire to obtain a word from this woman. I would have given my blood to hear the sound of Laurence's voice; all my being went out towards her, conjured her, begged her with clasped hands, to speak, to utter but a single syllable. I wept at her silence; a sort of vague uneasiness gained upon me as she became more sullen, more impenetrable. I felt myself gliding towards madness, towards a fixed idea; I had imperious need of a response; I made superhuman efforts, uttered prayers and threats, to obtain the satisfaction of this need which was devouring me. I multiplied my questions, emphasized my demands and changed the form of my interrogations, rendering them more urgent; I had recourse to all my gentleness, to all my violence, imploring, ordering, speaking in a caressing and submissive tone, then allowing myself to be carried away by anger, and afterwards making myself more humble, more insinuating still. Laurence, without a quiver, without a glance, seemed to ignore my presence. All my will, all my furious desire, to make her speak broke against the pitiless deafness of this creature who refused to listen to me.

This woman was escaping from me. I saw an insurmountable barrier between her and me. I held her form tightly clasped, I felt that form abandon itself with disdain to my embrace. But I could not open that soul and take possession of it; the heart and the mind had hidden themselves away; I pressed only a lifeless rag, so weary, so dull, that it was as nothing in my arms. And I loved this limp rag, I wished to keep it. I clung with despair to the sole creature who remained to me in the world, I exacted that she should belong to me, I had the fury of a miser when I thought that I was about to be robbed of her and that she was quite willing to allow herself to be stolen. I rebelled, I summoned all my strength to defend my own. And I was pressing a corpse to my bosom, an unknown thing which was a stranger to me and which I could not understand. Oh! brothers, you are ignorant of this suffering, of these bursts of love for an inanimate statue, of this cold resistance on the part of an adored being, of this silence in answer to so many sobs, of this voluntary death which might love, which one supplicates with all his eloquence and which loves not.

When my voice failed me, when I despaired of ever animating Laurence, I laid my head upon her breast, my ear against her heart. There, leaning on this woman, my eyes open, staring at the wick of the candle which was burning to a coal, I spent the night in thinking. I heard the rattle in Marie's throat, broken by fits of coughing, which came to me through the partition, lulling my thoughts.

I thought. I listened to the regular beating of Laurence's heart. I knew that nothing was there but a wave of blood; I said to myself that I was following in their rhythm the sounds of a well regulated machine, and that the voice which reached me was only the ticking of an unconscious clock, obeying a mere spring. And, nevertheless, I was disturbed; I would have liked to take the machine apart, to search out and study its most minute pieces; I thought seriously, in my delirium, of opening the breast upon which my head reposed, of removing the heart that I might see why it beat so gently and so regularly.

Marie's rattle continued, and Laurence's heart beat almost in my head. On hearing these two sounds, which were sometimes mingled together and made but one, I thought of life.

I know not why an insatiable longing for innocence pursues me in my abasement. I have constantly in my brain the thought of immaculate purity, lofty, inaccessible, and this thought awakens more biting in the depths of each of my fits of despair.

While I leaned my head upon Laurence's faded bosom, I said to myself that woman was born for a single love.

There is the truth, the only possible marriage. My soul is so exacting that it wishes all the creature it loves, in her infancy, in her sleep, in her entire life. It goes so far as to accuse dreams, so far as to declare that a sweetheart is guilty who has received in a vision the kiss of a shadowy adorer.

All young girls, even the purest and most sincere, have been the recipients of attentions from the phantom lovers of their dreams; those demons have held them in their arms, have made their innocent flesh quiver, have given them the first caresses. Hence, when they find husbands, they are no longer innocent, they no longer possess holy ignorance.

As for me, I wished my bride to come to me as she had left the hands of God; I wished her spotless, refined, not yet alive, and I would awaken her. She would live in me, she would know me alone, she would have no recollections save those which came to her through me. She would realize the divine dream of an eternal marriage of the soul and body, drawing everything from itself. But when a woman's lips have known other lips, when she has trembled like a leaf at the kisses of others, love can be nothing but daily anguish, hourly jealousy. Laurence does not belong to me, she belongs to her remembrances; she twists in my arms, thinking, perhaps, of former tendernesses; she is constantly escaping from me; she has a whole life which has not been mine; she and I are not one flesh. I love her and tear myself; I sob at the sight of this creature whom I do not possess, whom I can no longer possess in her entirety.

The candle smoked, the chamber was full of thick, yellowish air. I heard the rattling in Marie's throat, now coming to me through the partition in jerky sounds. I listened to Laurence's heart, but could not understand its language. This heart spoke, without doubt, an unknown tongue; I held my breath, I gave my intelligence altogether to it, but I utterly failed to grasp its meaning. Perhaps it was relating to me the past of my wretched and treacherous companion, her story of shame and misery. It beat slowly and ironically, letting the syllables fall from it with an effort; it made no haste to finish, it seemed to take delight in the recital of the horrible tale. I divined at times what it might be saying. I had ignored the past, I had refused to become acquainted with it, I had striven to forget it; but it voluntarily evoked itself, it presented itself to my mind such as it must have been. I knew what infamies it was necessary for me to imagine; but, amid the ignorance in which I had shut myself up, I, without doubt, went beyond the real and fell into a nightmare, exaggerating the evil. At this hour, I wished to know everything, to obtain a complete revelation of the truth in all its horror. I listened with the utmost attention to the cynical and heavy heart, which was narrating to me in a low voice and an unknown language the long and doleful story, but I could not follow the thread of the narrative, I could only imagine a few words which I thought I distinguished amid the unintelligible confusion of sounds.

Then, suddenly, Laurence's heart changed its language. It spoke of the future, and I understood it. It beat distinctly, talking more rapidly, with more violence, more irony. It said that it was going to the gutter and that it was in haste to arrive there. Laurence would quit me on the morrow, she would resume her life of chance; she would belong to the crowd, she would descend the few steps which yet separated her from the bottom of the sewer. Then, she would be a brute, she would no longer feel anything, and she would declare herself perfectly happy and contented. She would die some night upon the sidewalk, drunken and worn out. The heart told me that the body would go to the dissecting-room, and that the physicians would cut it to pieces to discover what bitter and nauseous things it contained. At these accursed words, I saw Laurence turned blue, dragged through the mud, covered with infamous stains, stretched out, cold and stiff, upon the white marble slab of the dissecting-table. The physicians were plunging sharp knives into the bosom of her I loved so much as to be ready to lay down my life for her, into the breast of the woman whom I held in my arms with the clutch of desperation.

The vision enlarged its scope; the chamber became filled with phantoms. A world of dissipation passed before me in a long, desolate procession. Life, with all its horrors and shames, presented itself to my eyes in a succession of frightful pictures. All the wretchedness of humanity arose before me, draped in silk, covered with rags, young and beautiful, old and bony. The parade of these men and these women, going to destruction, lasted a long while and filled me with terror.

The heart beat, beat. It said to me now, in anger:

"I came from the darkness of sin and shall return to it. You love me, but I shall never love you, for I am a dead heart and utterly worthless. You have striven vainly to make yourself infamous; you wish to descend to the mud, but the mud cannot ascend to you. You interrogate the silence, you endeavor to obtain light from darkness; you are trying to resuscitate an unknown corpse, which you would do better to carry immediately to the dissecting-table!"

I knew nothing further. The heart ceased to beat audibly, the burning wick of the candle was extinguished amid a flood of tallow. I remained leaning upon Laurence's bosom, fancying myself in the depths of some great black cavern, damp and deserted.

I still heard the rattle in Marie's throat.

XXIII

Practical Advice

This morning, on awaking, I had in me a glimmer of dolorous hope. The window had remained open, and I was as cold as ice.

I pressed my hands against my forehead; I said to myself that all this filth could not exist, that I dreamed at will of infamy. I had come out of a horrible nightmare; still shaken by the vision, I smiled as I thought it was only an illusion and that I was about to resume my calm life in the sunshine. I refused to entertain my recollections, I revolted, I denied. I had the indignation of honor.

No, it was impossible that I should suffer to this point, that life should be so wretched, so shameful; it was impossible that there existed such disgraces and such griefs.

I arose softly, and went to the window to breathe the morning air with all my strength. I saw Jacques below me; he was whistling tranquilly and gazing out into the courtyard. Then, the idea entered my mind to go down-stairs, to question him; he was a cold and just man who would calm my excitement, an honest man who would answer my questions with candor, who would tell me if he loved Laurence and what were his relations with her. By adopting this course, I might, perhaps, be cured. I would no longer feel that terrible warmth which was devouring my breast, I would trust Laurence, I would decide on a wise line of conduct which should release both her and myself from the desperate and wounding love into which circumstances had plunged us.

You see, brothers, that, though near the terrible dénouement, I still was hopeful. Oh! my poor heart, you are only a big child whom each hurt makes younger and warmer! As I passed Laurence, on my way to Jacques' apartment, I gazed for an instant at that slumbering girl, and, after so many tears, I again hoped to accomplish her reformation.

I found Jacques at work. He offered me his hand loyally, with a bright, frank smile upon his lips. I looked him straight in the face; I did not see in his peaceful features the treason I was searching for there. If this young man were deceiving me, he knew not that he was making my heart bleed.

"What!" cried he, with a hearty laugh, "are you no longer lazy? It is good for me, serious man that I am, to get up at six o'clock in the morning!"

"Listen, Jacques," I answered: "I am sick, and have come here to cure myself. I have lost consciousness of what surrounds me. I have lost consciousness of myself. This morning, on awaking, I realized that the sense of life was escaping from me, I felt myself lost in vertigo and blindness. This is why I have come down-stairs to grasp your hand, and to ask aid and advice from you."

I watched Jacques' face narrowly to note the effect of my words. He grew grave and lowered his eyes. He had not the attitude of a culprit, he had almost that of a judge.

I added, in a vibrating voice:

"You live beside me, you know the life I lead. I had the misfortune to meet, at the commencement of my career, a woman who has weighed me down and crushed me. I have kept this woman with me for a long while out of pity and justice. To-day, I love Laurence, I keep her beside me because I am madly, recklessly, devoted to her. I have not come here to ask you to employ your wisdom to effect a separation between her and me; I wish, if possible, for you to give me a last ray of hope by calming my fever, by making me see that everything in me is not shame. Do me the service of searching my being, of spreading it out bleeding before my eyes. If nothing good remains in me, if both my heart and my flesh are stained, I have fully resolved to sink myself, to drown myself, in the mud. If, on the contrary, you succeed in giving me a hope of redemption, I will make new efforts to get back to the light."

Jacques listened to me, shaking his head sorrowfully. I continued, after a brief silence:

"I do not know if you thoroughly understand me. I love Laurence with the utmost fury, I exact that she shall follow me in the light or in the mud. I should die of fear, if she left me alone in the depths of shame and misery; my heart will burst when I learn that, in her abasement, she has found other kisses than mine. She belongs to me in all her wretchedness, in all her ugliness. Nobody else would want the poor, abandoned and unfortunate creature. This thought makes her dearer, more precious to me; she is unworthy of anybody, I alone accept her; if I knew that another possessed my sad courage, my jealous rage would be all the greater because more love, more devotion, would be needed from him who stole Laurence from me. Therefore, do not argue with me,

Jacques; I have nothing to do with your ideas in regard to life, with your wishes and your duties. I am too high or too low to follow you in your path. You have a healthful mind; try only to assure me that Laurence loves me, that I love Laurence, that I ought to love her."

I had grown animated while speaking; I trembled, I felt madness growing upon me. Jacques, becoming graver and graver, sadder and sadder, looked at me and said, in a low tone:

"Child! poor child!"

Then he took my hands and held them in his, thinking, maintaining silence. My flesh burned, his was cool; I felt my visage contract, and I searched vainly in his, which remained grave and strong.

"Claude," said he to me, at last, "you are dreaming; you are beyond life, my friend, in the realms of nightmare and delusion. You have fever, delirium; your heart and your body both are sick. Amid your sufferings, you no longer see the things of this earth as they are. You give monstrous dimensions to gravel stones, you lessen the size of the mountains; your horizon is the horizon of vertigo, peopled by terrifying visions which are but shadows and reflections. I swear to you that your senses and your soul deceive themselves, that you see, that you love, what does not exist. My poor friend, I understand your disease, I even know the cause of it. You were born for a world of purity, of honor; you came to us without protection, without a guiding rule, your heart open, your mind free; you took immense pride in believing in the power of your tenderness, in the justice, the truth of your reasoning. Elsewhere, amid worthy surroundings, you would have increased in dignity. Among us, your virtues have hastened your fall. You have loved when you should have hated; you have been gentle when you should have been cruel; you have listened to your conscience and your heart when you should have listened only to your pleasure and your interest. And this is why you are infamous. The story is painful; you should consider yourself well punished for your pride, which urged you to live in defiance of the opinions of the crowd. To-day, your wound is bleeding, increased, irritated, by your own hands which tear it. You have maintained in your fall the impetuosity of your character: you desired to lose yourself utterly as soon as you felt the tip of your foot enter into evil. Now, you wallow, with holy horror, with the fury of bitter joy, in the ignoble bed upon which you have thrown yourself. I know you, Claude: you have been badly beaten, you do not wish to remain half conquered. Will you permit me, the practical man, the man without a heart, to endeavor to cure you by cauterizing your wound with a red hot iron?"

I made a gesture of impatience, opening my lips.

"I know what you are going to say to me," resumed Jacques, with more vivacity. "You are going to say to me that you do not wish to be cured, and that my red hot iron will not even make your already too much bruised flesh cry out. I know, besides, what you think, for I see your anger and your disdain. You think that we are worth less than you, we who do not love, who do not weep; you think that we have made this world, this woman who causes you to suffer, that we are cowardly, cruel, and that our way of being young is more shameful than your love and your abasement. You are on the point of crying out to me, to me who live tranquilly in the same mud as yourself, that you are dying of shame, that I lack soul if I do not die with you. You are, perhaps, right: I ought to sob, to twist my arms. But I do not feel the need of weeping; I have not your woman's nerves, your violence or your delicacy of sensation. I comprehend that you suffer through me, through the rest, through all those who love without love, and I pity you, poor, grown up infant, because you appear to me to suffer so much from an affliction I know nothing about. If I cannot ascend to you, cannot expose myself to your shame and pain arising from excess of soul and excess of justice, I wish, at least, in order to cure you, to give you our cowardice and our cruelty, to tear out your heart and leave your breast empty. Then, you will walk upright in the path of youth."

He had raised his voice; he grasped my hands strongly, almost with anger. This must be all Jacques' passion: a soulless passion, made up of logic and duty. Pale before him, my head half turned away, I smiled in contempt and anguish.

"Your Laurence," he continued, with energy, "your Laurence is a living disgrace! She is ugly, she is prematurely old, she is dangerous. Go up to your room and throw her into the street; she is ripe for expulsion! For more than a year, this girl has been a crushing burden to you; it is time that you had sent her off, that you had freed yourself, that you had washed your hands of her. I understand the weakness of pity; I might have sheltered Laurence for a time, if she had come to me begging for an asylum; but, on discovering the blackness of her heart, I would have returned to the sidewalk what belonged to the sidewalk, and I would have burned sugar in my chamber. Go up-stairs; throw her out of the window if she does not go quickly enough out of the door. Be cruel, be cowardly, be unjust, commit a crime. But, for the love of God, do not shelter a Laurence any longer. Such women are the cause of nine tenths of all the unhappiness in this world; they are makers of desolation and should be left to the mercy of the crowd; they deserve punishment, and it is not just to shield them from it. Do not persist longer in giving an asylum to this wicked wretch. You see that I am seeking some insult to exasperate you; I would render you worthy of your age by teaching you how to treat a Laurence, how to act like a practical man. For a year past, what have you done, except to weep? You are dead to work, you have lost caste, you do not look forward to the future. Laurence is the evil angel who has killed your intelligence and your hopes. You must kill Laurence. Hold, I have a last infamy to hurl in your face. You have not the right to live in poverty that you may shelter this woman; if you toiled, if you struggled, alone, you might die of hunger, but there would be a certain grandeur about your death. The few friends whom you had have left you; you saw them depart one by one, with coldness. Do you know what they say? They say that they cannot explain to themselves your manner of existence, that they cannot understand how you manage to shelter Laurence amid your poverty; the rich, when they give alms, say the same thing of the poor who have a dog. They say, those friends, that there is a method in what you do, and that you eat the bread which Laurence earns."

I escaped to my feet with a sudden movement, my arms closely locked against my breast. The insult had hit me full in the face; I felt a cold sweat cover my visage; I was stiff and icy; I no longer knew whether I was suffering or not. I had not believed that I had already fallen to this degree of abasement in the opinion of the crowd; I had desired a voluntary shame, but I had not desired insult. I drew back, step by step, towards the door, staring at Jacques, who also had arisen, and who was contemplating me with superb violence. When I stood upon the threshold, he said to me:

"Listen: you are going away without grasping my hand; I see that you will never forgive me for the wound I have just given you. While I am cowardly and cruel, I have something to propose to you. As I have tortured you, as I have excited your disgust, I must cure you. Send Laurence to me. I feel sufficiently courageous to separate her from you; to-morrow, your tenderness will be dead, you will then tell this woman she can no longer remain under the same roof with you. If you must have another love affair to hasten the work of consolation, go up-stairs, kneel beside Marie's bed and love her. She will not long be a burden to you."

He spoke with a cold anger, a lofty and disdainful conviction; he seemed to tread all love under foot, to walk over those women whom he entertained through capriciousness and custom; he looked straight before him, as if he saw his mature age congratulating him upon the logical shames of his youth.

So Jacques, the practical man, agreed with Pâquerette; both of them recommended to me an ignoble exchange, a remedy more distressing, more bitter, than the disease. I closed the door violently, and went up-stairs again, almost calm, stupid with grief.

There is, in the midst of despair, an instant when the intelligence escapes, when the events which succeed each other mingle together in dire confusion and no longer have any meaning. When I found myself once more before Laurence, who was still asleep, I forgot that I had just seen Jacques, I forgot both his advice and his insults; the heart and the mind of this man seemed to me gloomy abysses into which I could not descend. I was alone, face to face with my love, as yesterday, as ever; I had now but a single thought: to awaken Laurence, to clasp her in my arms, to compel her to accept life and kisses.

I awoke her, I took her with fury in my arms, I clasped her with such force as to make her cry out. I had a dumb rage, an implacable will. I was weary of being a stranger to Laurence, of being ignorant of what was passing through her brain; I desired to know the secrets of her soul. I said to myself that then I should no longer be tormented by suspicions, that I would force her to love me by warming her heart with my caresses.

Laurence had not spoken to me for two whole days. Pain unlocked her lips. She struggled and cried out to me, in a sullen tone:

"Let go of me, Claude, you hurt me! What a strange idea to wake people by choking them!"

I knelt upon the floor, at the side of the bed, and stretched out my hands towards my tormentor.

"Laurence," I murmured, in a gentle voice, "speak to me, love me. Why are you so cruel? What have I done that your lips and your heart maintain silence. Be frank; make me suffer all my sufferings in an hour, or cast yourself into my arms and let us live happily. Tell me all, give full scope to your thoughts and your affections. If you do not love me, strike a deadly blow, crush me and depart. If you love me, remain,

remain, but remain upon my heart, close, close, and speak to me, speak to me constantly, for I am filled with fear when I see you mute and sad for entire days, staring at me with your dead eyes. I feel madness coming to me in this desert amid which you are dragging me; I grow dizzy as I lean over you, so full of deep obscurity, of silent horror. No, I cannot live another day in ignorance of your love or your indifference; I wish you to explain yourself at once, I wish you, at last, to make yourself known. My mind is weary of searching; it is filled with sad solutions which it has formed of the problem of your being. If you do not desire my heart and my head to burst, name yourself, tell me what you are, assure me that you are not dead, that you still have blood sufficient to love or to hate me. I am reckless. Listen: we will set out to-morrow for Provence. Do you remember the tall trees of Fontenay? In Provence, beneath the glowing sun, the trees are prouder, stronger. We will live a life of love on that ardent soil, which will restore you your youth and give you a dark, passionate beauty. You shall see. I know, in a ravine sown with fine grass, a small, retired house, all green on one side with ivy and honeysuckles; there is a hedge, as tall as a child, which hides the ten leagues of the valley, and one sees only the blue curtains of the sky and the green carpet of the path. It is in this ravine, this nest, that we will love each other; it shall be our universe, and we will forget there the life we have led in the gloomy depths of this miserable chamber. The past shall be obliterated; the present alone, with its broad sunlight, its fruitful nature, its strong and gentle loves, shall exist for our hearts. Oh! Laurence, in pity speak to me, love me, tell me that you wish to follow me!"

She remained sitting up in bed, tranquilly wiping her eyes heavy with sleep, straightening out her hair, stretching her limbs. She yawned. My words seemed to produce upon her only the effect of disagreeable music. I had uttered the last sentences with so many tears, with such desperation, that she ceased to yawn and stared at me with an air at once vexed and friendly. She heaped the covers upon her bare feet; then, she crossed her hands and said:

"My poor Claude, surely you are ill. You behave like a child, you demand things of me which are anything but droll. I wish you only knew how much you fatigue me with your continual embraces, with your strange questions! You nearly strangled me the other day, now you weep, you kneel before me, as if I were the Holy Virgin! I comprehend nothing of all this. I never knew a man in the slightest degree resembling you. You are always stifling me, asking me if I love you. Of course, I love you, but you would do better, instead of making yourself sick here, to look for some work which would enable us to eat a little oftener. Such, at least, is my opinion."

She stretched herself out lazily, and turned her back to me, in order not to have in her eyes the light from the window which prevented her from going to sleep again. I remained on my knees, my forehead against the mattress, broken by the new burst of excitement which had just carried me away; it seemed to me that I had lifted myself too high and that, a hard and cold hand having pushed me, I had fallen headlong from the immensity of the heavens. Then, I remembered Jacques; but the remembrance appeared to me distant and vague: I would have sworn that years had elapsed since I had heard the terrible words of the practical man. My heart silently admitted to itself that this man was, perhaps, right in his selfishness: I felt a sudden temptation to take Laurence in my arms and carry her to the nearest street corner, there to throw her down and leave her.

I could not remain thus between Jacques and Laurence, between my love and my sufferings. I needed pacification, resolution; I needed to complain and to question, to hear a voice answer me and give me certainty.

I ascended to Pâquerette's room. I had never before entered the apartment of this woman. The chamber is on the eighth floor, immediately under the roof; it is a small mansarde and receives the light through a slanting window, the sash of which is lifted by means of an iron button. The wall paper hangs in blackish strips; the pieces of furniture—a bureau, a table and a bed of spun-yarn—lean one against another, in order not to fall. In a corner, there is a violet wood étagère, with threads of gold along the veneering, loaded with glassware and porcelain. The den is dirty, encumbered with damaged kitchen utensils full of greasy water; it exhales a strong odor of scraps of food and musk, mingled with a thousand other nameless and disgusting smells.

Pâquerette was gravely taking her ease in a red arm-chair, the covering of which, worn thin in spots, showed the wool with which the back and arms were stuffed. She was reading a little yellow book, full of stains, which she closed and placed upon the bureau when I made my appearance.

I took her hands, I wept. I seated myself on a stool, at her feet. In my despair, I was tempted to call her mother. I told her how I had passed the morning; I repeated to her the words of Jacques, those of Laurence; I emptied my heart, avowed my love and my jealousy, asked for advice. With clasped hands, sobbing, supplicating, I addressed myself to Pâquerette as to a good soul who knew life, who could save me from the mud into which I had blindly strayed.

She smiled as she listened to me, tapping me upon the cheeks with her withered and yellow fingers.

"Come, come," said she, when emotion had choked my voice in my throat, "come, you have shed enough tears! I knew that one day or another you would climb up here to ask aid and succor of me. I expected you. You took all this much too seriously; you should have reached sobs gradually. Do you wish me to speak frankly to you?"

"Yes, yes," I cried; "frankly, brutally."

"Well, you fill Laurence with fear! In the past, I would have shown you the door at the second kiss: you embrace too strongly, my son. Laurence remains with you, because she cannot go elsewhere. If you wish to get rid of her, give her a new dress!"

Pâquerette stopped With satisfaction at this phrase. She coughed, then pushed from her forehead a curl of gray hair which had just slipped over it.

"You ask advice from me, my son," added she. "I will give you through friendship the advice which Jacques gave you through interest. He will willingly deliver you from Laurence."

She laughed wickedly, and my pain became more intense.

"Listen," said I, with violence: "I came here to be calmed. Do not overturn my reason. Jacques cannot love Laurence after the words he spoke to me this morning, it is impossible."

"Ah! my son," answered the old woman, "you are very innocent, very young. I know not what you mean by love, and I know not if Jacques loves Laurence. What I do know is that they embrace each other in out-of-the-way corners. In the past, how many kisses I gave without knowing why, how many kisses were given to me which came from I know not where! You are a strange fellow, who do nothing like the rest. You should not have thought of having a sweetheart. If you are wise, this is what you will do: you will accept things as they are, and quietly Laurence will depart. She is no longer young; she may become a charge to you. Think of that. If you retain her, you will repent of it later. You had better let her go, since she herself wishes to take her departure."

I listened with stupor.

"But I love Laurence!" I cried.

"You love Laurence, my son; well, you will love her no longer! That is the whole of it. People unite and people quit each other. Such is life. But, great heavens! whence come you? How could such a man as you conceive the idea of loving anybody? In my time, people loved differently; it was then easier to turn the back than to embrace. You can readily understand that it is henceforward impossible for you to live with Laurence. Separate from her politely. I do not advise you to accept Marie as your sweetheart; that poor girl displeases you, and I think you had better jog on through life alone!"

I no longer heard Pâquerette's voice. The thought that Jacques might have deceived me in the morning had not before occurred to me; now, I plunged into it, not succeeding in believing it, but finding a sort of consolation in saying to myself that he had, perhaps, lied to me. This was a new shadow upon my mind, a new torment added to the torments which were already racking me. I was on the point of losing my senses.

Pâquerette continued, speaking through her nose:

"I wish to form you, Claude, to communicate to you my experience. You do not know how to love. One must be kind to women; one must not beat them, one must give them sweet things. Above all, no jealousy; if you are deceived, allow yourself to be deceived; you will be better loved afterwards. When I think of my adorers, I recall a little flaxen haired fellow who boasted that he had had for sweethearts all the girls of the public balls. Do you see that étagère, the last souvenir which remains to me? It came from him. One evening, he approached me and said to me, with a laugh: 'You are the only one whom I have not adored. Will you accept me after all the rest?' I accepted his homage, he kissed me upon both cheeks, and we supped together. That is the way to love."

I recovered from my stupor; I stared about the place in which I found myself. Then only I saw the filth of the den, then only I perceived the odor of musk and scraps of food. All my excitement had subsided; I realized the shame of my presence at the feet of this old wretch. The words which she had spoken to me, and which my memory had retained, grew clear and frightful in my mind, which before had turned them over without understanding them.

I had not the strength to go down-stairs to my chamber. I seated myself upon a step and wept away all the blood of my heart.

XXIV

Sad Reflections

I am a coward; I suffer and I dare not cauterize the wound. I feel that Pâquerette and Jacques are right, that I cannot live amid the frightful torment which is rending me. I must, if I do not wish to die of it, tear love from my bosom. But I am like the dying who are frightened by the unknown and the annihilation of the body. I know what is the anguish of my heart, full as it is of Laurence; I know not what would be its pain were this woman to leave it empty. I prefer the sobs of my agony to the death of my love; I recoil before the mysterious horrors of a soul widowed by affection.

It is with despair that I feel Laurence escaping from me. I press her in my arms like a horse hair shirt which brings the blood, which gives me a bitter delight. She tears me, and yet I love her. I love her for all the darts she drives into my flesh; I experience the painful ecstasy of those monks who die beneath the rods with which they strike themselves. I love and I sob. I do not wish to refuse to sob, if I ought to refuse to love.

And yet I realize that this sharp and biting nightmare must come to an end. The crisis is approaching. I do not know which of us is going to die. It seems as if anguish kept me awake, warned me of a coming misfortune. Heaven will take pity on me: it will cure my mind and leave me my heart; it will choose me for death rather than choose my tenderness.

This morning, I met a young man and a young woman, who were walking in the bright sunshine. With arms closely locked, they advanced slowly, forgetting the crowd. The young woman leaned her head upon the young man's shoulder; she gazed at him, moved and smiling, while he, in a glance, returned her emotion, her smile. This youthful couple absolutely sparkled with devotion and happiness, with pure love and genuine delight.

True youthful love then exists. While I live miserably in the deep gloom, torn and devoured by a horrible nightmare, a fearful incubus, there are, amid the sunbeams of May, true lovers who live deliciously. I did not know that people could love each other thus, I believed that kisses must of necessity be biting and poignant.

ÉMILE ZOLA

But, I remember now. Young lovers stroll along, two by two, in the moonlight, amid the first streaks of dawn. They are clad in light garments. They embrace each other at every step in a tender, dreamy fashion; they live amid the grass, among the crowd, and they are always alone. Heaven smiles upon them, the earth is discreet, the universe is their accomplice. Young lovers exchange their hearts, they live in each other's lives.

As for me, I am shut up here. I cannot have everything. I have the tears, the despair, of solitary love; I have the silence, the dead eyes, of Laurence. What need have I of spring and youthful love? I have my grief, if others have their joy.

Oh! my God, have pity! Do not deprive me of my suffering. Prevent this woman from curing me by killing my love. Let her remain where she is, at my side; let her remain there, cold and indifferent, to prolong my torment. I no longer know why I love her; I love her, setting aside all justice and all truth; I love her for the delight of loving her, and I do not wish to be disturbed amid the reckless madness of my devotion. My entire being is crushed by the idea that she may quit me; I am afraid of the dire desolation into which her absence would surely plunge me. In losing her, I would lose my family, all my affection, everything which yet binds me to this earth. My God, do not permit her to abandon me!

XXV

The Fair

L ast evening, in order to obtain partial relief from my sufferings, I strolled upon a fair ground. The faubourg was all gayety, and the people in their Sunday clothes were noisily passing through the streets.

The lamps had just been lighted. The avenue, at regular distances, was ornamented with yellow and blue posts, which were garnished with small, colored pots, and in these pots were burning smoky wicks, the flame and smoke being whirled about by the wind. In the trees Venetian lanterns swung. Canvas booths bordered the sidewalks, allowing the fringe of their red curtains to trail in the gutters. The gilded faïences, the freshly painted bonbons and the tinsel everywhere displayed shone in the raw light of the lamps.

There was in the atmosphere an odor of dust, of spiced cake and of greasy waffles; the powdered girls who led reckless lives laughed and wept beneath a hailstorm of kisses, blows and kicks. A hot and stifling mist hung over and weighed down upon this scene of riotous joy.

Above this mist, above these noises, spread out a cloudless sky, with pure and melancholy depths. An angel had lighted up the azure fields of the heavens for some divine fête, some majestically calm fête of the infinite.

Lost amid the crowd, I felt the solitude of my heart. I walked on, following with my glances the giddy young girls who smiled upon me as they went by, and I said to myself that I should never again see their smiles. This thought of so many loving lips, dimly seen for an instant and then lost forever, gave my sad soul, already tortured by my uncertainty in regard to Laurence, an additional pang of anguish.

In this wretched frame of mind, I reached a point where a street crossed the avenue. To the left, supported by an elm tree, stood an isolated booth. In front of it, a few badly joined planks formed a species of staging, and two lanterns illuminated the door, which was simply a bit of canvas raised like a curtain. As I came to a stop, a man wearing a magician's costume, a flowing black robe and a pointed hat sown with stars, was haranguing the crowd from the plank platform.

"Enter," cried he, "enter my fine Messieurs, enter my beautiful Demoiselles! I have come in hot haste from the furthest extremity of India to make young hearts rejoice. It was there that I conquered, at the peril of my life, the Mirror of Love, which was watched over by a horrible dragon. My fine Messieurs, my beautiful Demoiselles, I have brought you the realization of your dreams. Enter, enter, and see the person who loves you! For two sous you can behold the person who loves you!"

An old woman, clad like a bayadère, lifted the canvas door. She looked around upon the crowd with a stupid glance; then, she cried out, in a thick voice:

"For two sous, for two sous, you can behold the person who loves you! Enter and see the person who loves you!"

The magician beat a furious fantaisie upon a huge drum. The bayadère bent over a bell and accompanied him.

The people hesitated. A learned ass playing cards excited lively interest; a Hercules lifting weights of a hundred livres each was a spectacle of which no one would ever weary; neither is it to be denied that a half-clad giant was made to agreeably amuse those of all ages. But to see the person who loves you appeared to be the thing of which the crowd thought the least, and which they imagined did not promise them the slightest emotion.

As for me, I had eagerly listened to the summons of the man with the flowing robe. His promises responded to the desire of my heart; I saw a Providence in the chance which had directed my steps hither. The miserable mountebank had acquired a singular importance in my eyes, from the astonishment which I felt at hearing him read my most secret thoughts. It seemed to me that I saw him fix flaming glances upon me, beating the huge drum with a diabolical fury, crying out to me to enter in a voice which rose above the clash of the bell.

I had placed my foot upon the first plank step when I felt myself stopped. Turning around, I saw in front of the platform a man who had grasped me by the coat. This man was tall and thin; he had large hands covered by thread gloves larger still, and wore a hat which had grown rusty, a black coat whitened at the elbows, and deplorable cashmere pantaloons, yellow with grease and mud. He bowed almost to the ground, in a long and exquisite reverence; then, in a soft, sweet voice, he addressed to me this discourse:

"I am very sorry, Monsieur, that a well-bred young man like you should set the crowd such a bad example. It is a great shame to encourage in his impudence that wretch there, who is speculating upon our evil instincts, for I find profoundly immoral those words screamed out in the open air which summon the girls and the lads to mental and visual dissipation. Ah! Monsieur, the people are weak. We, the men whom instruction has made strong, have, believe me, grave and imperious duties to perform. Let us not yield to culpable curiosity, let us be worthy in all things. The morality of society depends upon us, Monsieur."

I listened to his speech. He had not released my coat and could not decide to finish his reverence. With his hat in his hand, he spoke with such polite calmness that I could not think of getting angry with him. I contented myself, when he paused, with staring him in the face without replying. He saw a question in this silence.

"Monsieur," resumed he, with a new bow, "I am the friend of the people and my mission is the well-being of humanity."

He uttered these words with a modest pride, suddenly lifting himself to his full height. I turned my back upon him and mounted the platform. Before entering, as I lifted up the canvas curtain, I looked at him again. He had delicately taken in his right hand the fingers of his left, striving to efface the folds of his gloves which seemed upon the point of slipping off.

Then, folding his arms, the friend of the people tenderly contemplated the bayadère.

I let the curtain fall and found myself within the temple. It was a sort of long and narrow chamber, without a single chair, with walls of canvas, lighted by a single lamp. A few persons—curious girls and lads making a great noise—were already assembled there. Setting aside the noise, the utmost propriety was observed: a rope, stretched across the middle of the apartment, separated the men from the women.

The Mirror of Love, to tell the truth, consisted simply of two looking-glasses without amalgam, one on each side of the rope, small round glasses through which could be seen the interior of the booth. The promised miracle was accomplished with admirable simplicity: it sufficed to apply the right eye to one of the glasses, and beyond, without either thunder or sulphur, appeared the loving person. Who could refuse to believe in a vision so natural!

I did not feel the strength to try the power of the Mirror of Love immediately after entering. I had a vague fear that I would see Marie. As I passed into the booth, the bayadère threw a glance at me which froze my heart. What awaited me behind that glass? Should I see

Laurence, who on the instant would change to some horrible monster, with sunken eyes and violet lips, a terrible vampire thirsting for youthful blood, one of those frightful creatures which I see at night in my evil dreams?

I was afraid, brothers; I retired into a corner. To recover courage, I looked at those who, bolder than myself, consulted destiny without so much hesitation. I experienced a singular pleasure at the sight of those different faces, the right eye wide open and the left closed with two fingers, having each its smile according as the vision pleased more or less. The glass was placed a little low; it was necessary to bend slightly, in order to look through it. I could not imagine anything more grotesque than the men coming up in single file to see the mates of their souls through a circular glass a few centimètres in circumference.

First, two soldiers advanced: a sergeant, browned by the sun of Africa, and a young conscript, having still the odor of the fields about him, his arms embarrassed by a cloak three times too large for him. The sergeant gave a skeptical laugh. The conscript remained bent for a long while, singularly flattered by having a sweetheart.

Then came a fat man in a white vest, with a red and bloated face, who gazed tranquilly without a grimace either of joy or displeasure, as if he thought it altogether natural that he should be loved by some one.

He was followed by three schoolboys, youths from fifteen to sixteen years old, with brazen mien, pushing each other to make people think that they had the honor to be intoxicated. All three of them swore that they saw their aunts in the Mirror of Love.

Thus, brothers, the curious followed each other before the mirror, and I cannot now recall the different expressions of countenance which struck me then. Oh! oh! vision of the well-beloved! what rude truths you spoke to those wide open eyes! They were the true Mirrors of Love, mirrors in which woman's grace was reflected in a dubious light, where luxury spread out into folly.

The girls, on the other side of the rope, amused themselves in a most genuine fashion. I read only intense curiosity upon their faces, I did not see the indication of the least wicked thought. They came, turn by turn, to throw an astonished glance upon the mirror and retired, some a trifle thoughtful, others laughing like so many fools.

To speak the truth, I know not what business I had there. If I were a woman, provided I was pretty, I would never entertain the foolish idea of putting myself out to go see the man who loved me. The days when my heart should weep at being alone, if those days were days of spring and golden sunlight, I would go into a flowery path that each passer-by might gaze at and adore me. In the evening, I would return rich with love.

The curious girls before me were not all equally pretty. The handsome ones derided the science of the magician; for a long time past they had had no need of him. The ugly ones, on the contrary, had never found themselves at such a fête as this. There came one of these, with thin hair and large mouth, who could not tear herself away from the magic mirror; she kept upon her lips the joyous and heart-rending smile of a poor wretch satisfying her hunger after a long fast.

I asked myself what fine ideas had been awakened in these foolish heads. This was not an easy problem to solve. All of them had, without doubt, seen in their dreams princes cast themselves at their feet; all of them desired to become better acquainted with the lovers whom they remembered so confusedly on awaking. There were, certainly, many deceptions; princes are becoming rare, and the eyes of our souls, which open at night upon a better world, are eyes much more accommodating than those we employ during the day. There were also great delights: the dream was realized; the lover had the handsome moustache and the black hair seen in the vision.

Thus each one, in a few seconds, lived a life of love, innocent romances, swift as hope, which one guessed from the blushes on the cheeks and the quivers of the corsages.

After all, these girls were, perhaps, fools, and I was a fool myself to have seen so many things where there was, doubtless, nothing whatever visible. Nevertheless, I completely reassured myself by studying them. I noticed that both men and women seemed in general thoroughly satisfied with the apparition. The magician, certainly, had never been malicious enough to give the least displeasure to these good folks who had paid him two sous.

I approached, brothers; I applied, without too much emotion, my right eye to the Mirror of Love. I perceived, between two huge red curtains, a woman leaning against the back of an arm-chair. She was brilliantly illuminated by lamps which I could not see, and stood out in relief against a piece of painted canvas, stretched across the end of the booth; this canvas, cut in places, must formerly have represented a fine grove of blue trees!

Brothers, I saw neither Marie nor Laurence. She who loved me, according to the magician's glass, wore, like a well-bred vision, a long white robe slightly fastened at the waist, flowing upon the floor like a cloud. She had across her forehead a wide veil, also white, held in place by a crown of hawthorn flowers. Thus clad, the dear angel was all whiteness, all innocence.

She leaned coquettishly against the back of the arm-chair, turning towards me large, caressing blue eyes. She seemed to me superb beneath the veil: she had flaxen tresses which were lost amid the muslin, a frank and pure forehead, delicate lips, dimples which were nests for kisses. At the first glance, brothers, I took her for a saint; at the second, I saw she had the air of a good girl and was not in the least conceited.

She lifted three fingers to her lips, and sent me a kiss, with a courtesy which did not in the least suggest the realm of shadows. Observing that she was not disposed to fly away, I fixed her features in my memory and retired from the mirror.

As I was quitting the booth, I saw my acquaintance, the friend of the people, enter. This grave moralist, who seemed to shun me, hastened to set the bad example of culpable curiosity. His long spine, bent in a semi-circle, shook with emotion; then, being unable to get nearer, he kissed the magic glass.

I descended the three plank steps of the platform; I found myself again in the crowd, decided to seek the girl who loved me now that I knew her smile.

The lamps smoked, the tumult was increasing, the people pushed along with such reckless haste that they nearly overturned the booths. The fête was at that hour of ideal joy in which, in order to be happy, one risks being suffocated.

On straightening myself up, I had before me a horizon of linen caps and silk hats. I advanced, pushing the men, cautiously getting around the great skirts of the women. Perhaps the girl who loved me was wrapped in that pink cloak; perhaps her head was beneath that tulle hood ornamented with mauve ribbons; perhaps she wore that delicious straw hat with an ostrich feather in it. Alas! the owner of the cloak was sixty; the hood, which concealed an abominably ugly face, leaned lovingly upon the shoulder of a sapper; she who wore the hat was laughing heartily, opening widely the most beautiful eyes in the world—but I did not recognize those beautiful eyes.

Brothers, above crowds hover I know not what anguish and what sorrow, as if the multitude had sent up a breath of terror and pity. Never do I find myself amid a great assemblage of people without experiencing a vague uneasiness. It seems to me that some frightful misfortune menaces these assembled men, that a single flash of lightning will suffice, amid the excitement of their gestures and voices, to strike them with motionlessness, with eternal silence.

Little by little, I decreased my pace, looking at this joy which wounded me. At the foot of a tree, in the full yellow light of the lamps, an old beggar was standing, his body stiffened, horribly twisted by paralysis. He lifted towards the passers-by his pale face, winking his eyes in a lamentable fashion the better to excite pity. He gave to his limbs sudden quivers of fever which shook him like a withered branch. The young girls, fresh and blushing, passed laughingly before this hideous spectacle.

Further away, at the door of an inn, two workmen were fighting. In the struggle, the glasses had been overturned, and to see the wine flowing over the pavement one might have thought it blood from great wounds.

The laughter seemed to me to be changed into sobs, the lights became a vast conflagration, the crowd whirled as if stricken with terror. I walked on, with a feeling of horrible sadness at my heart, staring at the faces of the young girls but never finding the person who loved me.

I saw a man standing before one of the posts which bore the lamps, considering it with a profoundly absorbed air. From his disturbed looks, I thought he was seeking the solution of some grave problem. This man was the friend of the people.

Having turned his head, he noticed me.

"Monsieur," said he to me, "the oil employed in fêtes like this costs twenty sous a litre. In a litre is enough to fill twenty lamps like those which you see there: hence each lamp consumes a sou's worth of oil. Now, this post has sixteen rows of eight lamps each: a hundred and twenty-eight lamps in all. Besides—follow my calculations closely—I have counted sixty similar posts in the avenue, which makes seven thousand six hundred and eighty lamps and, consequently, seven thousand six hundred and eighty sous, or, in other words, three hundred and eighty-four francs."

While speaking thus, the friend of the people gesticulated, emphasizing the figures, bending down his tall body as if to bring himself within the reach of my feeble understanding. When he paused, he threw himself back triumphantly; then, he folded his arms, looking me in the face with a penetrating air.

ÉMILE ZOLA

"Three hundred and eighty-four francs' worth of oil," cried he, putting a pause between each syllable, "and the poor people are without bread, Monsieur! I ask of you, and I ask it of you with tears in my eyes, if it would not be more honorable for humanity to distribute these three hundred and eighty-four francs among the three thousand indigent people contained in this faubourg? Such a charitable measure would give to each one of them about two sous and a half's worth of bread. This thought is well calculated to make tender souls reflect, Monsieur."

Seeing that I stared at him curiously, he continued, in a drawling voice, the while securing his gloves on his hands:

"The poor man should not laugh, Monsieur. He is altogether dishonest if he forgets his poverty for an hour. Who then will weep over the misfortunes of the people, if the government often gives such saturnalias as this?"

He wiped away a tear and left me. I saw him enter the shop of a wine merchant, where he drowned his emotion in five or six glasses of claret, taking one after the other over the counter.

The last light of the fair had just been extinguished; the crowd had dispersed. In the vacillating brightness of the street lamps, I now saw wandering beneath the trees only a few dark forms, couples of belated lovers, drunkards and sergents de ville airing their melancholy. The booths stretched away, gray and silent, on both borders of the avenue, like the tents of a deserted encampment.

Brothers, the morning breeze, damp with dew, imparted a quiver to the leaves of the elm trees. The biting emanations of the evening had given place to a delicious coolness. The softened silence, the transparent gloom of the infinite, fell slowly from the depths of the sky, and the fête of the stars followed the fête of the lamps. Honest people, at last, could amuse themselves a little.

I felt myself thoroughly rejuvenated, brothers, the hour of solitude having arrived. I walked with a firm step, ascending and descending the neighboring streets; then, I saw a gray shadow glide along the houses. This shadow came rapidly towards me, without seeming to see me; from the lightness of the step and the rhythmical rustle of the garments, I recognized a woman. She was about to run against me, when she instinctively raised her eyes. Her visage was revealed to me by the glimmer of a neighboring lantern, and I recognized it immediately as belonging to the girl who loved me: she was not the immortal in the white muslin cloud as I had seen her in the booth, but a poor daughter of this earth clad in faded calico. In her poverty, she seemed to me more charming than before, though pale and fatigued. I could not doubt the evidence of my senses: I saw before me the large eyes, the caressing lips of the vision, and, besides, I distinguished, on inspecting her thus closely, that sweetness of the features imparted by suffering.

As she stopped for a second, brothers, I seized her hand and kissed it, forgetting Laurence. She raised her head and smiled vaguely upon me, without seeking to withdraw her fingers. Seeing me remain silent, emotion having choked the words in my throat, she shrugged her shoulders and resumed her rapid walk.

I ran after her, caught her by the arm, and walked beside her. She laughed almost silently; then, she shivered and said, in a low voice:

"I am cold: let us hasten along."

Poor child, she was cold! Beneath her thin black shawl, her shoulders trembled in the cool morning breeze. I said to her, gently:

"Do you know me?"

Again she raised her eyes, and, without hesitating, replied: "No."

I know not what rapid thought shot through my mind. In my turn, I shivered.

"Where are you going?" I asked.

She shrugged her shoulders, and said to me, in a childish voice, with a little, careless pout:

"I am going home."

We walked along down the avenue.

I saw upon a bench two soldiers, one of whom was discoursing gravely, while the other listened with respect. These soldiers were the sergeant and the conscript. The sergeant, who seemed to me greatly moved, made me a mocking salute, murmuring:

"The rich lend, sometimes, Monsieur."

The conscript, a tender and innocent soul, said to me, in a tone full of grief:

"I had only her, Monsieur: you are stealing from me the girl who loves me!"

I crossed the thoroughfare, and took another street.

Three youths came towards us, holding each other by the arm and singing very loudly. I recognized the schoolboys. The little wretches had no further need to feign intoxication. They stopped, almost bursting with laughter; then, they followed me a few steps, crying after me, each one in an uncertain voice:

ÉMILE ZOLA

"Ho! Monsieur, Madame is deceiving you: Madame is the person who loves me!"

I felt a cold sweat moisten my temples. I hastened my steps in my eagerness to flee, thinking no more of the woman I was dragging along on my arm. At the end of the avenue, as I was about at last to quit this accursed spot, on stepping down from the sidewalk, I ran against a man who was sitting at his ease upon the curbstone. He was leaning his head against a lamp-post, his face turned towards the sky, and was executing with the aid of his fingers a very complicated calculation.

He turned his eyes, and, without moving his head from his pillow, stammered out:

"Ah! it is you, Monsieur! You must help me to count the stars. I have already found several millions of them, but I am afraid I have forgotten one somewhere. The welfare of humanity, Monsieur, depends upon statistics alone!"

A hiccough interrupted him. He resumed, with tears in his eyes:

"Do you know what a star costs? Surely, the great God has gone to vast expense on high, and the people lack bread, Monsieur! Of what good are those lamps up there? Can they be eaten? What is the practical application of them, I beg of you? We have no need whatever of this eternal fête!"

He had succeeded in turning his body around; he gazed about him with perplexed looks, tossing his head with an indignant air. It was then that he noticed my companion. He gave a start, and, with purple visage, greedily stretched out his arms.

"Ah! ah!" he stuttered, "it is the person who loves me!"

The girl and I walked on a short distance.

"Listen," said she: "I am poor; I do what I can to get something to eat. Last winter, I spent fifteen hours a day bent over my work, an honest trade, and yet I was sometimes without bread. In the spring, I threw my needle out of the window. I had found an occupation less fatiguing and more lucrative.

"I dress myself every evening in white muslin. Alone in a sort of nook, leaning against the back of an arm-chair, I have nothing to do but smile from six o'clock until midnight. From time to time, I make a courtesy, I send a kiss into space. For this I am paid three francs a sitting.

"Opposite me, behind a little glass enclosed in the partition, I incessantly see an eye looking at me. Sometimes it is black, sometimes blue. Without this eye, I should be perfectly happy; it spoils the business for me. At times, from always finding it alone and steadily fixed there, I am filled with wild terror, I am tempted to cry out and flee!

"But one must work for one's living. I smile, I courtesy, I send my kiss. At midnight, I wash off my rouge and resume my calico dress. Bah! how many women, without being forced to do so, air their graces before a mirror!"

By this time, we had reached the wretched abode in which this girl dwelt. I left her at the door, and returned to my mansarde and my misery.

ÉMILE ZOLA

XXVI

At Marie's Bedside

I take a sad pleasure in being in Marie's chamber. In the morning, I go there and sit upon the edge of the dying girl's bed; I live there as much as possible, departing with regret. Everywhere else, I belong to Laurence, everywhere else, I am feverish, excited and tormented. I hasten to reach this spot of pacification, I enter it with the feeling of confidence and comfort experienced by an invalid who is going to breathe a milder atmosphere, by which he expects to be cured.

I love death. The chamber is lukewarm, damp; the light there is gray and softened, made up of shadow and white brightness; everything there floats in a final languor, in a soft and dreamy half transparency. One does not know how sweet to a bleeding heart is the silence which reigns in a chamber where a young girl is dying. This silence is a strange, peculiar silence, full of exquisite mildness, full of restrained tears. The sounds—the clink of a glass, the crackling of a piece of furniture—are subdued, drag along like half stifled complaints; the cries from without enter in murmurs of pity, of compassionate encouragement. Everything is held in check, noise as well as light; everything is filled with grief and hope. And, in the shadow, amid the silence, one hears a vague despair which comes from one knows not where, and which accompanies the broken breath of the dying girl.

I gaze at Marie. I feel myself penetrated, little by little, by that invisible breath of consoling pity which fills the chamber. My eyes rest from their tears in that pale brightness; my ears, amid the quivering silence, forget for an hour the sound of my sobs. All the gentleness, all the delicate attentions, all the faintly uttered and caressing words, intended for Marie, seem as if addressed to me; they subdue the sound of voices and footsteps; they question, they reply, affectionately; they avoid sharp and painful sensations; and, as for me, I believe, at times, that all these considerate precautions are taken that my poor being, full of suffering, may not burst asunder. I imagine that I am dying, that they are taking care of me; I seize my share of the care and consolation; I steal from Marie half of her agony and of the pity it causes; I go there, beside a dying girl, to profit by the regrets and tenderness which men accord to the last hours of a soul. I am curing my love through death.

I feel that it is the need of being pitied, of being caressed, which pushes me into this chamber. I find here the atmosphere, the pity, necessary for me. Life is too sharp for my painful flesh and my wounded heart; the bright sunlight irritates me; I am at ease only in the restorative seclusion of the tomb. If, some day, I emerge from my despair, I ought to thank God for having permitted me to live thus, seated at the foot of a bed of death, for having allowed me to share the pacification of a dying creature. I will live, because a child expired at my side.

I gaze at Marie. The fever purifies her flesh from day to day. She is growing younger, she is becoming a little girl, amid the exhaustion of her blood. Her deeply sunken face expresses an ardent longing, the longing for the end, for rest; her eyes are enlarged, her pallid lips remain half open as if to facilitate the passage of the final breath. She is waiting, resigned, almost smiling, as ignorant of death as she has been ignorant of life.

Sometimes, we look each other in the face for long hours. I know not what thought then arrests the cough upon her lips; she seems filled with a single idea, which suffices to keep her awake, to give her more life and more calmness. Her countenance grows tranquil, pink flushes appear upon her cheeks; her limbs beneath the bed clothes have less stiffness; Marie, under the influence of my glance, stretches herself out, shakes off the iron grasp of death. As for me, I am absorbed in her, I share her sufferings; little by little, it seems to me that I pass in through her half open lips and that I become a part of this sick creature; I experience a gentle and bitter sensation at languishing with her, at slowly sinking away; I feel the inexorable disease take possession of my entire body, shake me with increasing violence, in proportion as my glances penetrate deeper and deeper into those of Marie; I say to myself that I shall die simultaneously with her, and a great flood of joy sweeps through me.

Oh! what strange fascination and what wonderful pacification I experience! Death is powerful; it has biting temptations, irresistible attractions. One must not lean over the eyes of a dying creature, for they are full of light and so deep that their abysses make one dizzy. One wishes to see what those enlarged eyes behold, one is seized with frightful curiosity in regard to the unknown. Every time Marie looks at me, I desire to die, to leave this world with her, in order that I may know what she will know; I imagine that she is soliciting me, that she is begging me not to abandon her, that she is dreaming we will go away in company, taking the risk of the same annihilation or the same splendor.

Then, I forget, I forget Laurence. Though I see Laurence in everything, waking or sleeping—in the objects which surround me, in that which I eat and in that which I drink—I do not see Laurence in the depths of Marie's eyes. I see there only that blue glimmer, paler now, which I saw one night while my lips touched the poor child's lips. That blue glimmer does not speak to me of my love, does not speak to me of my grief; it is the only thing at which I can gaze without weeping. This is the reason I love Marie's chamber, this is the reason I love the dying girl with her dilated eyes which have more purity, more gentleness, than the sky, for the sky, when I lift my face towards it, speaks to me of Laurence. I am about to lose myself in this oblivion, in this clear and serene light which is so pure. Perhaps, thereby, my heart will be cured.

When the night comes on and I can no longer see the blue glimmer in Marie's eyes, I open the window, I gaze at the black wall. The square patch of yellow light is there, empty or peopled, still and sad or filled with silent movements. I feel a sharp sensation on finding myself again, after several hours of forgetfulness, face to face with reality, face to face with my jealousy and my anguish. Every evening, I recommence the painful and colossal task of giving a meaning to those dark stains which increase in size and roll in a bewildering way over the surface of the wall. I have converted this search into a dolorous recreation. I apply myself to it with an anxious patience, an obstinacy full of fever, and each night I am drawn back to the window, though I promise myself daily that I will no longer risk my reason there.

XXVII

Marie's Death

I have reached that plenitude of despair which is almost rest. I cannot suffer additionally; this certainty that nothing can augment my tears is a solace. My being has torn itself to such an extent that it has stopped in pity. To-day, I can only wipe away my tears.

And yet I feel that I have need of Heaven to be cured. I have the brutishness of pain, I have not the tranquil joy of health. If my wounds cannot be enlarged, they cannot remain open, bleeding drop by drop, with inexorable suffering.

Brothers, the hand which is to close them is a terrible hand, the hand of death and truth.

Yesterday, when night came on, Marie's chamber was filled with gloom and silence. A candle, half hidden behind a vase on the mantelpiece, lighted a corner of the ceiling; the walls and the floor were in darkness; the bed was white amid the transparent shadows. Marie, paler, more broken, had closed her eyes. I knew that she could not last through the night. Pâquerette was asleep in her arm-chair, her hands crossed in her lap, smiling in a dream at some imaginary gluttony; her chin resting on her corsage, she was snoring softly, and the sound of her breath mingled with the weakened rattle in Marie's throat. I felt myself suffocating between this dying young girl and this old woman gorged with food. I hastened to the window. I opened it. The weather was clear.

I leaned my elbows upon the sill, and gazed at the square patch of yellow light on the wall opposite. The stains came and went with rapidity, fading away to re-appear of greater dimensions than before. Never had the shadows been so nimble, so ironical; they seemed to be indulging with delight in a jeering dance, in an inexplicable confusion of shapes, wishing to entirely overthrow my reason. It was an indescribable pell-mell, a mass of heads, necks and shoulders, which rolled upon itself as if beaten and flattened by the strokes of a flail. Then, suddenly, at the very instant when I was smiling bitterly, no longer seeking to understand, supreme quietness settled down upon the sombre and agile shadows; the stains gave a final leap, two profiles were thrown upon the wall, enormous, full of energy, standing out with sharpness and vigor. It seemed as if, weary of tormenting me, the shadows had at last decided to reveal themselves; they were there, black, powerful, full of superb truth and insolence. I recognized Laurence and Jacques, out of all proportion, disdainful. The two profiles approached each other slowly and united with a kiss.

I had not ceased to smile. I felt in myself a sort of tearing sensation, followed by a sudden feeling of satisfaction. My heart, with an enormous pulsation, had driven out all the love which was stifling it, and that love had gone out through my veins, giving me a final burn. I felt that sensation of anguish which the patient experiences beneath the hands of the surgeon: I suffered in order that I might cease to suffer.

At last, the shadows had spoken, they had given me a certainty. I had the truth written there, before me, upon the wall; I knew that which I had sought to guess for so many long days; I stared fixedly at those two black heads, which were kissing in the square patch of yellow light.

I was astonished at suffering so little. I had thought I should die on learning the truth, and I felt only an extreme lassitude, a benumbing of all my being. For a long while, I remained leaning upon my elbows, staring at the two shadows which were agitating themselves in a curious fashion, and I thought of the terrible episode which was finished by the kisses of two dark stains upon an illuminated wall. The conversation which I had had with Jacques then returned forcibly to my memory; in the gulf which had opened within me I heard, repeated one by one, gravely and slowly, the words of the practical man, and those words, which I imagined I was listening to for the first time, astonished me strangely, uttered in the presence of the kisses which the shadow of Jacques was giving to the shadow of Laurence. Who was deceived in all this? Was Pâquerette right, or was I staring at one of those inexplicable caprices of the mind, which urge people to lie to themselves? Could it be possible that Jacques was devoting himself to save me, going as far as deceptive caresses? Singular devotedness, which could strike me in my flesh, in my heart, and cure me of an evil by an evil more terrible still!

Little by little, my thoughts grew troubled, I no longer possessed the calmness of the first moment.

I could not comprehend those kisses, and, at last, I began to fear that what I had seen was only a miserable trick.

The struggle between doubt and certainty was, for an instant, re-established within me, sharper, more biting, than ever. I could not imagine that Jacques loved Laurence; I believed more in him than I believed in Pâquerette. Then, I said to myself that kisses have their intoxication, and that he would learn to love this woman, if he did not love her already, by applying his lips to her lips in that fashion.

Hence I suffered anew. My jealousy was reawakened, my anguish again took me by the throat.

I should have retired from that window, I should not have abandoned myself to the sight of those two shadows. What I suffered in a few minutes cannot be told; it seemed to me that they had torn out my heart and that I could not weep.

The truth was clear, inexorable: little did it matter whether Jacques loved or did not love Laurence; Laurence hung upon his neck, gave herself to him, and she was henceforward dead for me. There was the sole reality, the dénouement at once desired and feared.

Amid the horrible torture which racked my being, I felt everything crumble away within me; I realized that I was now without faith, without love; I went back to Marie's bed and knelt beside it, sobbing.

Marie awoke, she saw my tears. She made a superhuman effort, and, quivering with fever, sat up in bed. I saw her bend down, leaning her head upon my shoulder, I felt her wasted and burning arm encircle my neck. Her eyes, luminous amid the darkness, full to overflowing with the brightness of death, questioned me with fright and compassion.

I would have liked to pray. I had need of clasping my hands, of imploring a kind and compassionate Divinity. I felt myself weak and deserted; in my childish fear I wanted to give myself to a good God, who would take pity on me. While Jacques was tearing Laurence from me and while the guilty couple, below me, were indulging in loving kisses, I had an overwhelming desire to make my profession of faith and love, to protest on my knees, to love elsewhere, in the light, before all the world. But my lips were ignorant of prayer, I despairingly stretched out my arms, in space, towards the mute sky.

I encountered Marie's hand, and pressed it gently. Her dilated eyes were still questioning me.

"Oh! let us pray, my child," said I to her, "let us pray together."

She seemed not to understand me.

"What is the matter with you?" murmured she, in a faint and caressing voice.

And her feeble hand sought to wipe away my tears. Then, I looked at her and my torn heart melted with pity. She was dying. She was already beyond life, whiter, grander; her glassy eyes were filled with

ÉMILE ZOLA

a soft and serene ecstasy; her tranquil countenance was as if wrapped in slumber, her thin lips no longer emitted the rattle. I realized that she was about to die in my arms, at this solemn hour when my tenderness was also dying, and her agony, mingled with that of my love, filled my soul with compassion so deep that I again stretched out my hands into space with a more biting anxiety, searching for some one.

I lifted myself up, and, in a low, broken voice, repeated:

"Let us pray, my child, let us pray together."

Marie smiled.

"Pray, Claude?" said she. "Why do you wish me to pray?"

"To console us, Marie, to obtain pardon for us."

"I have no pardon to ask for, I have no sorrow to be softened. See, I am smiling, I am happy; my heart reproaches me with nothing."

She was silent for a moment, putting aside her locks from her forehead; then she resumed, in a weaker tone:

"I know not how to pray, because I have never had to ask for pardon. The woman who brought me up assured me that the wicked alone went to church to obtain absolution for their crimes. I am a child who never did evil; never have I had need of God. Whenever I wept, my tears flowed copiously down my cheeks and the wind dried them. Do you wish me to pray for you, Claude?" added she, after another period of silence. "You shall clasp my hands and make me repeat the words which they teach to the children in the villages. I will ask God not to make you weep any more!"

Trembling, touched, I prayed for Marie, I prayed for myself. I found in the depths of my being words of supplication and adoration, and I uttered them one by one without moving my lips. I supplicated Heaven to be merciful, to make death easy, to put this child to sleep in her ecstasy, in her ignorance. And, while I prayed, Marie, without seeing that I was addressing God, clung to my neck with greater force, bending over my face.

"Listen, Claude," said she; "I will get up to-morrow, I will put on a white dress and we will leave this house. You will find a little chamber in which we will shut ourselves up all alone. I plainly see that Jacques loves me no more, because I am too weak, too white. You have a kind heart; you will take good care of me and I will live with more happiness, more gayety, than ever before. I am a trifle weary, I have need of a kind brother. Will you be that brother, Claude?"

These words, uttered with languishing tenderness, were horrible in the mouth of the dying girl. She preserved her innocent shamelessness even in the arms of death; she offered herself upon her dying bed as a sister and a sweetheart of ten years of age. I supported her poor body as if its flesh had been sacred, I listened to her ardent and low voice with a holy compassion.

I thought, no longer being able to pray. What then is evil? Was I not in the presence of absolute good? Surely, God created everything sinless, everything perfect. Evil is one of our inventions, one of the wounds with which we are covered by reason of our own iniquity. This child who was dying was no more disturbed, in life, by the kisses she had given her admirers than a little girl is disturbed by the caresses which she gives her doll. And Laurence, sad and desolate Laurence, showed such degradation that her shamelessness was no more than the tacit acceptance of a purely material act. Where shall we find the evil in all this, and who would dare to punish Laurence and Marie, the one for her brutishness, the other for her ignorance? The heart had fallen asleep, or had not yet been awakened. It could not be the accomplice of the flesh, which itself remained innocent in its silence. If I had had to condemn these two women, I would have had more tears than severity, I would have desired for them death, supreme peace.

They ought to sleep very soundly in their tombs, these poor creatures who have lived amid tumult and feverish gayety. Perhaps, nevertheless, their hearts will love at last in death, suffering frightfully at the thought of a life passed in loving without love; they would struggle now, but they are nailed in their coffin. Marie was departing, white and pure, astonished, quivering, realizing, perhaps, that she was dying before having known life. I wished that she could take with her Laurence who had no more to learn, having exhausted every pleasure. They would both descend into the unknown with the same step, equally soiled, equally innocent, daughters of God bruised by men.

I was supporting Marie's head, which was weighed down with agony.

"Where is Jacques?" she asked.

"Jacques," I replied, "is with Laurence. They have abandoned us; we are alone."

"Alone! Has Laurence left you, Claude?"

"Yes. She has left me. We are alone."

She gently rubbed her hands one against the other.

"Oh! it is good, oh! it is good to be alone," murmured she; "we can live under the same roof. They have done well to arrange matters in this way. We owe them our thanks. May they be happy on their side; we will be happy on ours."

Then, she assumed a tone of confidence, and said, in a low and joyous voice:

"You never knew it, but I did not like Laurence. She was bad to you; she made you shed tears which I would willingly have dried. At night, I could not sleep; I was rude even to Jacques; I wished to ascend to your chamber to watch over you, in order that she might not harm you. You will never leave me again, will you, Claude? I will be a good little woman, and will take up as small a space as possible."

Marie maintained silence for a short time, smiling at her thoughts. She was growing weaker and weaker, she was becoming inert. I supported her form, I felt the life quitting her flesh with every word she uttered. She had now but a few minutes to live. Her smile faded away, she seemed to be stricken with fear.

"You are deceiving me, Claude," she suddenly resumed: "Laurence is not in Jacques' chamber. You are trying to please me. Have you ever seen him kiss her?"

"Yes."

"Where?"

"Over there, opposite, upon the wall."

Marie clasped her hands.

"I wish to see," said she, pressing against me.

She had a hollow and supplicating voice; she caressed me, humbly and gently.

I took her in my arms and lifted her from the bed. She was very light, all palpitating; she abandoned herself to my grasp. I carried her cautiously, scarcely feeling her weight, fearing to hurt her. My hands touched with a holy respect this poor, dishevelled creature, who clung to my neck, belonging already to death.

When, with outstretched arms I held her before the window, Marie, whose head was thrown back, looked at the sky. The heavens were of a deep blue, sown with stars; the calm air was full of warm, slow quivers. The eyes of the dying girl were fixed upon the stars, she breathed the lukewarm air. Her visage, until then resigned, had a painful contraction, like a revolt of the expiring flesh in the presence of the breath of life. She was absorbed in her contemplation, her glance wandered about in the sombre space, she seemed to be dreaming her last dream.

I heard her murmur and bent down. She said:

"I do not see them, they are not kissing."

And she gently agitated her poor hands in the air, as if to tear away the veil which was stretched before her sight.

Then, I lifted up her head. The shadows, in the square patch of yellow light, were still kissing. They were blacker, more energetic, and their sharpness made them frightful. Marie saw them.

A glad smile showed itself upon her lips. With childish joy, with a youthful voice, she approached my ear, caressing me with her hand.

"Oh! I see them, I see them," she said. "They are kissing. They have enormous heads, all black. I am afraid. Tell them that we are together, that they must come no more to torment us. One night they kissed each other thus; we also kissed on our side, and it was from that moment that I no longer liked Laurence. Do you remember that night? Come closer that I may kiss you. It will be our second kiss, that of our betrothal."

Marie tremblingly placed her mouth against mine. I felt pass between my lips a breath accompanied by a slight cry. The body which I held in my arms had a convulsion, then relaxed.

I glanced at Marie's eyes. They were wide open, but I searched vainly for the blue glimmer which had burned in them on that night of which she had just spoken.

Marie was dead, dead in my arms.

I carried back the corpse and laid it upon the bed, carefully covering the body which until then I had held against my bosom. I sat down upon the edge of the bed, I leaned the head of the child upon one of my arms, holding her hands, looking at her face which yet seemed to live and smile. She was taller in death, more serene, purer.

Great tears, flowing down my cheeks, fell amid the hair of the dead girl, which covered my knees.

I know not how long I remained thus, amid the silence and the darkness. Suddenly, Pâquerette awoke, she saw the corpse. She arose, all in a tremble, and ran to get the candle behind the vase upon the mantelpiece; then, when she had held the flame before Marie's lips and had realized that all was, indeed, over, she gave vent to noisy despair. This old woman recoiled with fright from death which she felt beside her; she cried out with grief as she thought that she also must soon die. She had never believed in the sickness of this poor girl, who seemed to her too young to have departed so quickly; before the rapid and terrible dénouement she trembled with terror. Her cries must have been heard in the street.

A sound of footsteps came from the stairway. Some neighbor was ascending, attracted by Pâquerette's exclamations.

The door opened; Laurence and Jacques appeared upon the threshold.

Oh! brothers, I cannot continue the frightful narrative to-day. My hand trembles, my eyes are filled with gloom. To-morrow, you shall know all.

XXVIII

Laurence's Departure

Laurence and Jacques, confused and frightened, appeared upon the threshold of the door.

Jacques, on seeing Marie's corpse, clasped his hands in terror and astonishment. He had not expected such a sudden death. He hurried to the bed, knelt down at its foot, and buried his face in the sheet which was on the point of falling to the floor. Deep anguish seemed to be crushing him. He did not stir. I could not tell whether he was weeping or not.

Laurence, pale, her eyes dry, remained upon the threshold, not daring to advance. She quivered and turned away her glances.

"Dead! dead!" she murmured, in a low voice.

And she took two or three steps, as if to see the better. Then, she stood still in the middle of the chamber, alone.

As for me, I yet held the corpse in my arms, I covered myself with it, I protected myself against Laurence who was approaching.

"Do not advance," cried I to her, harshly, "do not come here to soil this child who is sleeping. Remain where you are. I have to judge and condemn you."

"Claude," she answered, in a meek voice, "let me kiss her."

"No, no, your lips are all bruised with Jacques' kisses. You would profane the dead."

Jacques seemed to be asleep, his head in the sheet. Laurence fell upon her knees.

"Listen, Claude," she said, stretching out her hands towards me: "I know not what you see upon my lips, but do not speak to me with such harshness. I have need of gentleness."

I stared at this woman, who was humbly complaining, and I failed to recognize Laurence. I clasped Marie closer, fearing some weakness.

"Arise and listen to me," I cried out to Laurence: "I wish to make an end of this. You come from Jacques' room. You should not have come here. You opened the wrong door."

Laurence arose.

"Then, it is your intention to drive me away, is it?" asked she.

"It is not I who drive you away. You have driven yourself away by accepting another asylum. Remain in that asylum."

"I have not chosen another asylum. You are deceived, Claude. There are no strange kisses upon my lips. I love you."

She advanced timidly, fascinating, her arms outstretched.

"Do not approach, do not approach," I cried again, with a movement of fright. "I do not wish you to touch me, I do not wish you to touch Marie. The poor dead girl protects me against you; she is here, upon my breast, asleep; she calms my heart. I feel myself terribly torn. I should, perhaps, have had the baseness to pardon you, if you had come into our chamber and there dragged yourself at my feet, for there you would have been all-powerful over me, by reason of that infamous love with which misery and abandonment have inspired me. Here, you can exert no influence over my heart, no influence over my body. I still have upon my lips Marie's soul, her last breath and her last kiss. I do not wish your soiled mouth to take that soul from me."

Laurence paused, sobbing, gazing at me through her tears.

"Claude," murmured she, "you do not understand me, you have never understood me. I love you. I never knew what you wanted of me; I gave myself as I knew how to give myself. Why do you drive me away? I have done no evil; if you think I have done evil, you can beat me and we will still live in company."

I was weary, I felt my heart bleed; I was in haste to see this woman depart, I implored her in my turn.

"Laurence," said I, more gently, "in pity go away. If you have ever had any love for me, spare me further suffering. Our tenderness for each other is dead, we must separate. Go forth into life, where you will, but take the path that leads to goodness and happiness, if you can. Let me recover my hope and my gayety."

She folded her arms in despair, repeating several times, in a wild tone:

"All is over, all is over!"

"Yes, all is over," answered I, with emphasis.

Then, Laurence fell upon the floor in a mass, and burst into violent sobs.

Pâquerette, who had tranquilly resumed possession of her armchair, looked at her with curiosity. The old wretch was filled with astonishment, chewing some lozenges which she had just found, Marie not having lived long enough to finish the box.

"Ah! my child," said she to Laurence, "have you also lost your senses? Great heavens! what fools lovers are in these days! In my time, people quitted each other gayly. Do you not see that it is greatly to your advantage to separate from Claude. He consents. Thank him, and depart at once."

Laurence did not hear her, she was striking the floor with her feet and with her fists, a prey to a sort of nervous crisis. Lightly clad, she twisted, panting, full of quivers which shook her all over. She bit her hair which had fallen over her face, she uttered half stifled cries, confused words which were lost amid her sobs.

I saw her from head to foot, crushed and quivering; I felt neither pity nor anger.

Then, she got upon her knees, and, her face convulsed, her flesh reddened and blued by tears, dragging herself towards me in her twisted and hanging skirts, she cried out:

"You are right, Claude, I am bad. I prefer to speak the truth, to tell you everything. You will, perhaps, pardon me afterwards. Your eyes have rightly seen: my lips should be red with Jacques' kisses. I went to him, I forced him to treason. I am a wicked wretch!"

Her sobs convulsed her bosom. They mounted from the depths of her being in enormous and painful breaths, swelled her throat horribly, made her whole body undulate, burst from her lips in hollow and heart-rending cries.

"Have mercy upon me," murmured she. "I did not know that Jacques' kisses would separate us. I acted without reflection, without thinking of you. I grew weary sometimes, in the evening, when you came to this chamber. Then, I sought to amuse myself. That is the true state of the case; it admits of no other explanation. I do not wish to quit you. Pardon me, pardon me!"

At this last hour, this woman was more impenetrable than ever. I could not understand this creature, cold and weighed down, nervous and suppliant. For a year I had lived beside her, and yet she was as much a stranger to me as on the first day of our acquaintance. I had seen her turn by turn old and young, active and sluggish, cold and loving, cynical and humble; I could not reconstruct a soul with these diverse elements, I stood dumb before her dull and grimacing visage which hid from me an unknown heart. She loved me, perhaps; she yielded to that craving for love and esteem which is found in the depths of the most depraved natures. But I no longer sought to understand her; I realized that Laurence would always remain a mystery to me, a woman made up of gloom and vertigo; I knew that she would remain in my life like an inexplicable nightmare, like a feverish night full of monstrous and incomprehensible visions. I did not wish to listen to her, I felt myself still in a dream; I was afraid of yielding to the madness of the darkness, I yearned with all my strength for the light.

I made a movement of impatience, refusing with a gesture, firmly closing my lips. Laurence, fatigued, pushed her hair from her face; she looked straight at me, silent, disheartened, she no longer supplicated, for words had failed her. She begged me by her attitude, by her glance, by her disturbed countenance.

I turned away my head. Laurence then arose painfully, and went to the door without taking her eyes from me. She stood for an instant, straight, upon the threshold. She seemed to me to have grown taller, and I almost weakened, almost threw myself into her arms, on seeing that she wore, at this last hour, the ragged remains of her blue silk dress. I loved that dress, I would have liked to tear a rag from it to keep in remembrance of my youth.

Laurence, walking backwards, passed into the darkness of the stairway, addressing to me a final prayer, and the dress was now only a black flood which quiveringly glided over the steps.

I was free.

I placed my hand upon my heart: it was beating feebly and calmly. I was cold. Deep silence reigned within my being, it seemed to me that I had awakened from a dream.

I had forgotten Marie, whose head still peacefully reposed upon my breast. Pâquerette, who had been dozing, suddenly arose and laid the body upon the bed, saying to me as she did so:

"Look at the poor child! You have not even closed her eyes. She seems to gaze at you and smile."

Marie was gazing at me. She had an infant's sleep, a supreme peace, the forehead of a pure and sainted martyr. She seemed happy at what she had understood before her death, when she had said that we were alone, that we could love each other. I closed her eyes that she might slumber in this thought of love, and kissed her eyelids.

Pâquerette placed two candles upon a little table near the corpse; then she resumed her doze, curled up in her arm-chair. Jacques had not stirred; all my words, all those of Laurence, had passed over him without making him start. On his knees, his face buried in the sheet, he was absorbed in some harsh and terrible thought which overwhelmed him and deprived him of speech.

The chamber was now silent. The two candles sent forth a pale light, which whitened the bed clothes and Marie's uncovered face. Beyond this narrow circle of brightness, all was but uncertain gloom. Amid this gloom, I vaguely perceived Pâquerette asleep and Jacques kneeling. I went to the window.

I passed the night standing there, with a narrow bit of sky above me. I looked at Marie and I looked within myself; I towered above Jacques, I distinguished Laurence far off, very far off, in my memory. My mind was healthy, I explained everything to myself, I comprehended my being and the creatures who surrounded me. It was thus that I was enabled to see the truth.

Yes, Jacques had not been deceived. I was ill. I had fever, delirium. I feel to-day, from the fatigue of my heart, what must have been the violence of my disease. I am proud of my sufferings, I understand that I have not been infamous, that my despair was but the rebellion of my heart incensed at the society into which I had unwittingly brought it. I am awkward before shame, I cannot accept common love; I have not the tranquil indifference necessary to live in this corner of Paris, where beautiful youth wallows in the midst of the mud. I need the pure mountain summits, the broad country. If I had encountered a spotless girl, I would have knelt before her and given myself entirely to her; I would have been as pure as she, and, without struggle, without effort, we would have united our fortunes, we would have become husband and wife. Life has its fatalities. One night, I met Laurence with her throat uncovered; I was imprudent enough to shelter this woman, and at length I loved her, loved her as if she had been a spotless angel, with all my heart, all my purity. She repaid my affection with suffering and despair; she had had the baseness to allow herself to be loved without ever having once loved on her side. I tore myself, before this dead soul, in a vain attempt to make myself understood. I wept like a child who wishes to kiss his mother, standing on the tips of his little feet, but unable to reach the visage of her in whom all his hope is centred.

I said these things to myself during that supreme night, and I said to myself, besides, that some day I would speak and show the truth to my brethren, the hearts of twenty years. I found a great lesson in my wasted youth, in my broken love; my entire being cried out: Why did you not remain at home, in Provence, among the tall grass, beneath the glowing sunbeams? There you would have increased in honor, in strength. But, when you came here to seek life and glory, why did you not keep from the mud and pollution of this great city? Did you not know that man has neither two youths nor two loves? You should have lived like a well-ordered young man amid your work, and you should have loved some pure and spotless creature, not Laurence.

Those who accept without tears the life which I have led for a year past have no heart, those who weep as I have wept come out of that life with broken body and dying soul. The Laurences must be killed, then, as Jacques said, since they kill our flesh and our love. I am only a child who has suffered, I do not wish to preach here. But I show my empty breast, my wounded and bleeding body; I desire that my wounds may make the young men of my age tremble, and may arrest them on the edge of the gulf. To those who delight in brightness and purity I will say: "Take care, you are about to enter the gloom, the realm of temptation." To those whose hearts are asleep and who are indifferent in regard to evil I will say: "Since you cannot love, try at least to remain worthy and honest."

The night was clear, I saw far into the blue sky. Marie, now stiffened, slept heavily; the sheet thrown over her had long folds, sharp and hard. I thought of the annihilation of the flesh, I thought that we had great need of faith, we who live in the hope of to-morrow and who know not what to-morrow may bring forth. If I had had a God in Heaven, whose protecting arm I had felt about me, I should not, perhaps, have yielded to the vertigo of a wretched passion. I should always have had consolations, even in the midst of my tears; I should have employed my excessive love in prayer, instead of not being able to bestow it upon any one and feeling it stifle me. I had abandoned myself, because I had faith in myself only and had lost all my strength. I do not regret having obeyed my reason, having lived in freedom, having had respect only for the true and the just. But, nevertheless, when the fever seizes upon me, when I tremble with weakness, I am filled with fear, I become a child; I would prefer to be controlled by the Divine will, to efface myself, to allow God to act in me and for me.

Then, I thought of Marie, asking myself where was her soul at this hour. In the great realm of nature, without doubt. I indulged in the dream that each soul is merged in the grand whole, that dead humanity is but an immense breath, a single spirit. Upon earth we are separated, we are ignorant of each other, we weep at our inability to unite ourselves;

beyond life there is a complete penetration, a marriage of all with all, a single and universal love. I looked at the sky. I seemed to see in the calm and quiet stretch of blue the soul of the world, the eternal soul made up of all the others. Then, I experienced a great delight, I had shot ahead of my cure, I had arrived at pardon and faith. Brothers, my youth still smiled upon me. I thought that some day we would be reunited all four—Marie and Jacques, Laurence and myself; we will understand each other, we will pardon each other; we will love each other without having to hear the sobs of our bodies, and we will experience a supreme peace in exchanging those tendernesses which we could not give each other when we lived in the flesh.

The thought that there is a misunderstanding upon earth, and that everything is explained in the other world, consoled me. I said to myself that I would wait for death in order to love. I stood near the window, in the presence of the sky, in the presence of Marie's corpse, and, little by little, a gentle coolness, a limitless hope, came to me from that dead young girl and the dreamy space.

The candles had burned out. The silence in the chamber grew heavier and heavier, and the darkness increased. Pâquerette still slept. Jacques had not moved.

Suddenly he arose, he stared around him in terror. I saw him lean over the corpse and kiss it on the forehead. The cold flesh sent a shiver through him. Then, he noticed me. He came to me, hesitated, and then offered me his hand.

I looked at this man whom I could not comprehend, who seemed to me as obscure as Laurence. I did not know whether he had lied to me or whether he had wished to save me. This man had struck my heart a heavy blow. But I had recovered hope, I had pardoned. I took his hand and pressed it.

Then, he went away, thanking me with a look.

In the morning, I found myself beside Marie's bed, on my knees, still weeping, but my tears were mild, softened. I wept over this poor girl whom death had carried off in her spring, ignorant of the kisses of love.

XXIX

Conclusion

Brothers, I am coming to you. I set out to-morrow for the country, for Provence. I wish to draw a new youth from our broad horizons, from our pure and glowing sunbeams.

My pride has led me to aim at too lofty a mark. I believed myself ripe for the struggle, while in reality I was but a weak and inexperienced child. Perhaps, I shall always remain a child.

I rely upon your friendship, on my remembrances. Near you, I will recall the days of the past, I will quiet myself, I will succeed in curing my heart. We will go into the plains, on the shady bank of the river; we will resume the life we led when we were sixteen, and I will then forget the terrible year through which I have just passed. I will return to those days of ignorance and hope, when I knew nothing of reality and when I dreamed of a better earth. I will become young again, believing; I will recommence life with new dreams.

Oh! I feel all the thoughts of my youth return to me in a body, filling me with strength and hope. Everything had disappeared amid the gloom into which I had entered—you and the world, my daily toil and my future glory. I lived only for a single idea: to love and to suffer. To-day, amid my tranquillity, I feel awakening, one by one, those thoughts which I recognize and to which I extend a hearty welcome, with a softened soul. I was blind, but now I see clearly within me; the evil is torn away, I find the world as I left it, broad for youthful courage, luminous, full of applause. I will resume my labor, recover my strength, struggle in the name of my faith, in the name of my tenderness.

Make a place for me beside you, brothers, let us live in the pure air, in the fields sparkling with sunbeams, in our pure love. Let us prepare ourselves for life by loving each other, by going hand in hand in freedom beneath the blue sky. Wait for me, and make Provence sweeter, more encouraging, to receive me and restore me my childhood.

Last night, when at the window, in the presence of Marie's corpse, I purified myself with faith, I saw the sky, full of gloom, whiten at the horizon. All night long I had had before my eyes the black stretch of space, pricked by the yellow light of the stars; I had vainly sounded the infinity of the sombre gulf, growing terrified at the immense calmness, at the unfathomable depths. This calmness and these depths were lighted up; the darkness quivered and slowly rolled back, allowing its mysteries to be seen; the fear inspired by the gloom gave place to the hope inspired by the growing brightness. The whole sky grew inflamed, little by little; it acquired rosy tints as soft as smiles; it bathed in the pale light, sparkling with faint brilliancy. And, alone in the presence of this tearing away of the night, of this slow and majestic birth of the day, I felt in my heart a young, invincible strength, an immense hope.

Brothers, it was the dawn.

THE END

ÉMILE ZOLA

A Note About the Author

Émile Zola (1840–1902) was a French novelist, journalist, and playwright. Born in Paris to a French mother and Italian father, Zola was raised in Aix-en-Provence. At 18, Zola moved back to Paris, where he befriended Paul Cézanne and began his writing career. During this early period, Zola worked as a clerk for a publisher while writing literary and art reviews as well as political journalism for local newspapers. Following the success of his novel *Thérèse Raquin* (1867), Zola began a series of twenty novels known as *Les Rougon-Macquart*, a sprawling collection following the fates of a single family living under the Second Empire of Napoleon III. Zola's work earned him a reputation as a leading figure in literary naturalism, a style noted for its rejection of Romanticism in favor of detachment, rationalism, and social commentary. Following the infamous Dreyfus affair of 1894, in which a French-Jewish artillery officer was falsely convicted of spying for the German Embassy, Zola wrote a scathing open letter to French President Félix Faure accusing the government and military of antisemitism and obstruction of justice. Having sacrificed his reputation as a writer and intellectual, Zola helped reverse public opinion on the affair, placing pressure on the government that led to Dreyfus' full exoneration in 1906. Nominated for the Nobel Prize in Literature in 1901 and 1902, Zola is considered one of the most influential and talented writers in French history.

A Note from the Publisher

Spanning many genres, from non-fiction essays to literature classics to children's books and lyric poetry, Mint Edition books showcase the master works of our time in a modern new package. The text is freshly typeset, is clean and easy to read, and features a new note about the author in each volume. Many books also include exclusive new introductory material. Every book boasts a striking new cover, which makes it as appropriate for collecting as it is for gift giving. Mint Edition books are only printed when a reader orders them, so natural resources are not wasted. We're proud that our books are never manufactured in excess and exist only in the exact quantity they need to be read and enjoyed.

Discover more of your favorite classics with Bookfinity™.

- Track your reading with custom book lists.
- Get great book recommendations for your personalized Reader Type.
- Add reviews for your favorite books.
- AND MUCH MORE!

Visit **bookfinity.com** and take the fun Reader Type quiz to get started.

Enjoy our classic and modern companion pairings!